Hi, I'm Reshma. I'm the founder of Girls Who Code, where we teach middle- and high-school girls how to change the world by writing code. The girls in our coding clubs create all sorts of cool things, including games, apps, websites, and more.

Have you ever been in a talent show? I remember performing in one when I was in elementary school—my friends and I put together a Bollywood dance! Talent shows were always a ton of fun, but they were also a lot of work. Fortunately, I had a group of friends to practice with, and we always enjoyed ourselves, even if we didn't win.

In this book, you'll read about Erin and her BFFs in coding club—Maya, Sophia, Leila, and Lucy—getting ready for their school's talent show. But, even more exciting, they're developing a web app so that students can vote for their favorite performances online! I wish there had been a web app for our talent shows when I was growing up (apps weren't really a thing yet). That would have made talent shows even more exciting!

Erin also deals with a personal problem in this story, and is scared to tell her friends about it. But she soon learns that best friends can help you get through even the toughest times. Like the other books in our Girls Who Code series, this book is about—above all—the importance of sisterhood and having a supportive group of friends who are always there for you. That's one of the most vital things we teach in our programs at Girls Who Code.

If you like reading this book, I hope you'll join one of our free coding clubs across the country. In our clubs, you'll make amazing friends—and you might even create something you can use in a talent show one day.

Happy reading—and coding!

Reshma Saujani

PENGUIN WORKSHOP
Penguin Young Readers Group
An Imprint of Penguin Random House LLC

Penguin supports copyright. Copyright fuels creativity, encourages diverse voices, promotes free speech, and creates a vibrant culture. Thank you for buying an authorized edition of this book and for complying with copyright laws by not reproducing, scanning, or distributing any part of it in any form without permission. You are supporting writers and allowing Penguin to continue to publish books for every reader.

The publisher does not have any control over and does not assume any responsibility for author or third-party websites or their content.

Emoji © denisgorelkin/Thinkstock, cupcake emoji (p. 132) © Aratehortua/iStock/Thinkstock.

Library of Congress Control Number: 2018016052

ISBN 9780399542541   10 9 8 7 6 5 4 3 2 1

by Michelle Schusterman

Penguin Workshop
An Imprint of Penguin Random House

Chapter One

My heart raced as I hurried down the corridor, glancing at my watch. First day back from spring break, and I was almost two minutes late for coding club—but I had a *really* good reason.

I burst through the door, and over the tops of the computers, all heads turned toward me. Only one way to handle a mildly embarrassing moment like this.

Doubling over, I clutched my sides. "Water," I wheezed. *"Water."*

Everyone started giggling. From the third row, I saw my coding club besties—Lucy Morrison, Sophia Torres, Maya Chung, and Leila Devi—laughing with the rest of the class. At the front of the room, Mrs. Clark smiled at me.

"Everything okay, Erin?"

I straightened, fanning my face with my hand. "Yes!

Sorry I'm late, but I have an announcement."

Mrs. Clark crossed her arms and leaned against her desk. "Funny, I have a few announcements myself. But why don't you go first?"

"Why *thank* you," I said, with an exaggerated bow that got more snickers from the class. Then I pulled a folded-up flyer from my jeans pocket. "I just saw Ms. Davies printing these." I held the flyer out for everyone to read the three words at the top, in a giant font:

ALL THE TALENTS!

"The talent show, yeah," said Bradley Steinberg. "Everyone already knows that's next Friday. I'm doing a stand-up act!"

I wiggled the flyer. "But this year, the film club is working with the theater club to do a different format. Everyone who wants to enter will make a video. And the talents can be anything, like animation or . . . or robot building!" I grinned at Leila, and her wide blue eyes lit up. Leila was super into robotics.

Then I pointed at Maya, our school's resident fashion expert. Her short black hair was swooped over to the right and pinned down with, like, a dozen star-shaped barrettes that matched the pattern on her purple leggings. "Or clothes you designed! It could be *anything*. And then everyone can watch the videos and vote!"

"Which was actually going to be my first announcement," Mrs. Clark said, smiling as she gestured for me to sit down. I hurried over to the empty seat between Maya and Lucy, as Mrs. Clark continued. "So it's true: This year's talent show is going to have a new format. Like Erin said, anyone who wants to enter can make a video, then upload it to our school's video platform. Then they can share them through a web app that all students will have access to. After everyone votes, the top three finalists will perform at an assembly a week from this coming Friday."

To my right, Lucy sat up straighter, one of her long, thick braids falling over her shoulder. "A web app?"

"That's right," Mrs. Clark said, eyes twinkling behind her glasses. "The film club will be compiling the videos, and our school already has the video platform, but the web app doesn't exist ... yet."

She raised her eyebrows meaningfully, and murmurs broke out.

"Do we get to design it?" Sophia asked eagerly. She'd turned away from her computer to stretch out her super-long legs, and I noticed her track shoes were extra muddy. Sophia lived with her parents, three sisters, and her grandmother (who'd moved here from Puerto Rico to help out), so she didn't usually have money for extras.

Mrs. Clark nodded. "It's a pretty big project with some tight deadlines. But I think you're all up for the challenge!"

"Awesome," Lucy said fervently. Maya and I exchanged a grin because Lucy looked like she'd just won the lottery. We all loved coding, but Lucy couldn't get enough of it. Her mother was a computer scientist—one of the first African American women at her company—and the apple hadn't fallen far from the tree.

And honestly, I was just as excited as Lucy about this project. I was definitely entering the talent show. Performing was 100 percent my thing. Or maybe 90 percent, because I had coding club and film club. One of the drawbacks of my interests, though, was that theater didn't fit into my schedule. I still missed being onstage.

Besides, even more fun projects to work on were exactly what I needed. Anything to keep me from thinking about The Thing I Wasn't Supposed to Think About.

As everyone logged into their computers, Maya leaned over and nudged me.

"So what's your act gonna be?"

I adopted a look of mock innocence. "What act?"

"Come on," Maya said teasingly. "There's no way you're not entering the talent show. Singing, dancing, doing impressions and silly voices—you actually *have* all the talents. Or, at least, a lot of them."

"Moi?" I gasped, placing a hand on my chest. On my other side, Lucy started chuckling. "Vhat are zees talents you speak of? Vhat zilly voices? Vhat dancing? Vhat—"

"Erin?"

I jumped, startled, and realized Mrs. Clark was looking at me. "Vhat? I mean, yes?"

"Mind if we get started?"

"But of course," I drawled, and Maya shook her head, grinning.

For the next ten minutes, Mrs. Clark explained more about how the web app would work. Students and teachers would register with their e-mail accounts to get access. Then contestants would upload a video, and anyone could view it if they were signed in. She started a task list on the board, and soon everyone was calling out suggestions.

"Web design," Maya said. *"All the Talents* sounds like a reality show—maybe we can make the web app look like it really is one!"

"Each student can only vote once, right?" Lucy chimed in. "We'll have to program it so that once you click on a vote button, you can't click on any others."

"There should be a notification system," added Maddie Lewis. "An easy way to let everyone know who the finalists are."

"Maybe we could program it to automatically send updates, too!" added her twin brother, Mark. "Like who's in the lead every day. That might get more kids to watch and vote."

The suggestions kept coming, and soon the board was filled with Mrs. Clark's writing. She hadn't been kidding—this was a *huge* project.

And then we had to spend another ten minutes figuring out which ideas we needed. Like we learned at the hackathon (a day of coding where teams won prizes at the end), adding too many things could create "feature creep" (when a project became impossible to use because it had too much going on). So we had to cut down the list. A lot.

After all that, though, we still had to start on the real work!

"Next step: splitting into groups and dividing up these tasks," Mrs. Clark said. Maya and I automatically scooted our chairs closer to Lucy. On her other side, Leila and Sophia did the same thing.

"Why split up a dream team?" I asked Mrs. Clark, and she laughed. It was true, though. We weren't just best friends; we were an awesome team, too—like at the hackathon in the fall, when our robot had turned the event into an epic dance party.

"Any of these tasks sound particularly interesting?" Mrs. Clark asked.

Lucy was gazing at the board. "I was thinking about the voting feature we're designing for the app," she said. "Could we make it so that students rank their top three favorites?"

Maya tilted her head. "Or, like, rank each contestant on different qualities? Creativity, originality . . ." Maya hadn't been so into coding club at the beginning of the school year, but she was totally into it now.

"That'd give us a *lot* of data," I pointed out. "Way more than if everyone just voted once for their favorite. We'd know *why* certain contestants were more popular than others."

Mrs. Clark was nodding. "It's certainly not necessary for the talent show to be a success, but it might be interesting to analyze that kind of data afterward! So, is this what your group wants to do?"

We all looked at one another eagerly. "Yeah, I think so!" Lucy said.

As Mrs. Clark moved on to the next group, I pulled out a notebook and pen. "I like Maya's idea about voting in different categories," I said, jotting it down. "What do you all think?"

"I think it's a great idea," Leila said, adjusting her head scarf. "It's easy to watch two contestants singing or dancing and just pick which one you think is best. But if contestants are going to be doing all kinds of stuff, like a stand-up act or—"

"Or a flying robot?" I interrupted, waggling my eyebrows.

Leila giggled. "Or that, yeah. It'd be harder to judge which one is better. Rating different qualities for each contestant seems more fair."

"What should the qualities be?" Sophia asked.

Maya had opened the browser on her computer and pulled up the website for a talent reality show. "These contestants are judged based on overall performance, technical ability, style and execution, and originality."

I scribbled in my notebook. "So if we use those qualities, our program will have to average them together for each contestant . . . but how? Ratings?"

"That might be confusing for people voting," said Lucy, tapping her pencil on her notebook. "I mean, what does three stars really mean? Why don't we make it even simpler: an upvote for each category? Like a thumbs-up you click on—and whoever gets the most thumbs-ups, wins."

"Is anyone else picturing the winner onstage, surrounded by hundreds of thumbs?" I asked with a perfectly straight face, and everyone giggled.

We spent the next half hour taking notes and brainstorming ideas for our voting feature. Then Mrs. Clark walked back to the front of the room and cleared her throat.

"It looks like you're all off to a great start," she said. "If you need any help this week, feel free to e-mail me. Now, before we leave, I actually have another announcement. Erin, you mentioned earlier that your group might be able to collect a lot of interesting data with your voting feature, right?"

I nodded, closing my notebook.

"That's actually something some people make a career out of," Mrs. Clark said. "They're called data scientists. Think about every time you use your phone or a computer, every time you click on a link or type something into a search box—you're creating data for these experts to analyze, and they learn all kinds of amazing things. That's actually what I did before I came to teach here, and I loved it."

Mrs. Clark was smiling, but in an almost sad sort of way, and a feeling of foreboding washed over me.

"Of course, I love teaching, too," she went on. "And teaching this club in particular. In fact, seeing how far you've all come since the beginning of the year, and your enthusiasm for coding—it's really inspired me to take on greater challenges." She paused, and gave a sweeping look at everyone. "So I was excited over spring break when TechTown offered me a job as a data scientist."

Next to me, Lucy gasped. "Wait, does this mean you're leaving school?"

Maya nudged Lucy with her elbow, but her eyes were wide, too.

"Not for a few weeks," Mrs. Clark said. "But yes, I accepted the job. Teaching this club has been so much fun, and I'm really going to miss you all. But I've talked to Principal Stephens, and I know he'll find a great replacement . . ."

She kept talking, but I stopped listening. My hands

were suddenly clammy, and my palms were starting to itch. It was a familiar feeling, although one I hadn't felt in years.

No, I told myself firmly. *No, that's not what this is. This is not a panic attack.*

My heart was pounding faster and faster, and soon a rushing sound filled my ears. I squeezed the edge of my chair and stared at my keyboard. The more I tried to convince myself I had no reason to have a panic attack, the more panicky I felt. Had my friends noticed? What about Mrs. Clark? Was the whole class staring at me?

I closed my eyes and focused on breathing slowly until my pulse finally started to slow down. The rushing sound went away, and I heard voices and the scratching of chair legs on the tile floor as everyone started to leave. There was a hand on my arm, and someone was saying my name.

"Huh?" I opened my eyes. Lucy was staring at me with a concerned look.

"Erin, are you okay?"

"Yeah!" My voice came out in a squeak. "Totally fine."

"I can't believe Mrs. Clark is leaving," Sophia groaned. "I mean, I'm happy for her. But ugh."

"Who do you think will replace her?" Maya adjusted

one of her star-shaped barrettes. "Should we go to the Bakeshop and eat all the cupcakes to make ourselves feel better?" Maya ate mostly Chinese food at home, which she loved, but she also loved cupcakes—who wouldn't?

"Yes!" Lucy said, already buttoning up her coat. "And we can work on this voting feature, too!"

I zipped up my jacket, trying to hide the fact that my fingers were still shaking. "I'd love to, but I promised my mom I'd come home right after coding club," I lied. "Sorry, guys."

"Aw, we'll miss you!" Sophia gave me a one-armed hug. I thought I saw Lucy give me another concerned look, although she didn't say anything. My friends chatted as we left the classroom, but I didn't say a word until we walked outside.

"See you tomorrow!" I called, waving and hurrying off in the opposite direction. My stomach was in knots, and not just because of Mrs. Clark's news. The Thing I Wasn't Supposed to Think About was there, too, constantly hovering in the back of my mind. I needed more distractions if I was going to stop the panic attacks from coming back.

Right now, that meant I had to bake.

Chapter Two

My recipe for red-velvet waffles with cream cheese glaze has a few secret ingredients: buttermilk so that the batter is extra creamy, crushed pecans to give it a crunch, and lemon zest to balance the sugary glaze with a little brightness.

But the one ingredient that can make or break the whole thing?

A waffle iron.

"Where *are* you?" I muttered, taking care not to bump my head on the sink pipes as I rummaged through stacks of pots and pans. "Come on, I know you've got to be in here somewhere . . ."

"Well, hello there, Erin's butt."

I giggled, shaking my backside a little before scooting out of the cabinet. My mom was setting her purse on the counter. She eyed the mess on the table—bowls filled with batter and glaze, flour and sugar and red food coloring spattered everywhere—and smiled at me.

"Red-velvet waffles? What's the occasion?"

"No reason," I said quickly, closing the cabinet door. "Just wanted a good snack. Any idea where the waffle iron is?"

"Hmm." Mom frowned as she poured a glass of iced tea. "I remember we kept it in the pantry in the last apartment, but in *this* apartment . . ." She took a sip and stared around the kitchen. Then her face brightened. "Wait. You haven't made waffles since we moved here, have you?"

And suddenly, I knew exactly where the waffle iron was. We both said it at the same time.

"Junk closet!"

I hurried out of the kitchen, crossed the living room, and stopped in front of the closet in the hallway. About a dozen boxes—some still taped up, some ripped open—were stacked haphazardly inside.

Every apartment we'd ever lived in had a junk closet, although it wasn't always an actual closet. One time it was the bathtub. (Don't worry, the shower was separate.)

It was never intentional. We just always hit a point during the unpacking process when we were too tired to finish. And we knew we'd be packing it all up again soon enough. So the boxes filled with stuff we didn't use on a daily basis got shoved into what we always called the junk closet.

A weird thought hit me as I dug through the boxes, looking for the waffle iron. This was the first apartment Mom and I had moved into with just the two of us. Now that Mom and Dad were divorced, Dad's military career didn't decide where we lived anymore . . . but we were still treating this apartment as if it were temporary.

"Aha!" Triumphantly, I pulled the waffle iron out from under an unopened box of stationery Aunt Lilith had given Mom for her last birthday. I brushed dust off its plastic top, then spotted what had been underneath it and froze.

"Brave Bonnie Broomstick!" I whispered.

A yellow teddy bear gazed up at me with slightly crooked button eyes. Her black cape was wrinkled, and her pointy witch hat was squashed. Tucking the waffle iron under my arm, I lifted her out of the box.

"How did *you* end up in the junk closet?" I asked, doing my best to straighten her hat. I didn't remember packing her. Actually, I couldn't even remember the last time I'd seen her. Dad had given me Brave Bonnie Broomstick the first time he'd been deployed.

"A very brave witch-bear," he'd told me. "For a very brave witch-girl."

(That was when I was going through my witch stage. No one could pull off a gray wig and snaggly teeth like first-grade me.)

I smiled at Bonnie, and my eyes welled with tears. Uh-oh. I was definitely thinking about The Thing I Wasn't Supposed to Think About. And I definitely didn't want Mom to see me crying because she'd immediately know why. And *then* we'd have to talk about it. Wiping my face with the back of my hand, I took a few deep breaths before heading back to the kitchen.

"Mom, you'll never guess what I—hey!"

Mom looked up guiltily, her finger still in the bowl of red-velvet batter. "Whoops. Caught red-handed." She licked the batter off and grinned. "Or red-fingered, I guess. Hey, is that . . ."

"Brave Bonnie Broomstick!" I exclaimed, wiggling the bear in Mom's face. "She was under the waffle iron. I think one of her eyes is a little loose."

"Aw," Mom replied. "I could sew it on tighter, if you

like. Or, you know, we could yank it off and go for the classic one-eyed witch look."

Forcing a laugh, I plugged the waffle iron in next to the coffeemaker. "Option number one, please," I said, flipping the switch to on. "Hey, do you think it's weird that we still have a junk closet?"

Mom handed me the bowl of batter. "Huh, I hadn't thought about it. Do *you* wanna unpack those boxes?"

I wrinkled my nose. "Uh, I was thinking you'd do a better job. You know, with your extra-awesome organizational skills."

We both chuckled. Mom was good at lots of things, like being a social worker, typing at lightning-fast speed, and singing along with the *Grease* cast album in this super-dorky way that made me cry with laughter every time. But being organized was *not* one of her strengths.

"Well, at least we can find a permanent home for the waffle iron now." Mom watched as I tested the iron's heat by dropping a bit of batter onto the griddle. When it sizzled, I poured a ladle's worth on, closed the lid, and set the timer.

"And Brave Bonnie," I said, poking her lovingly on the nose. "She doesn't deserve to live in a box."

Mom took another sip of iced tea. "Yeah? Where's her new home going to be?"

"My room, of course!" I set down the bowl and started taking out the plates and forks. A few seconds passed before I realized Mom was watching me with that *how-do-I-say-this* expression she gets right before awkward conversations.

"So Brave Bonnie's back," she said at last. "Honey, does this have anything to do with your dad's mission?"

Aaaaand there it was. The Thing I Was Definitely Thinking About Now.

The military called them "training missions." But they were very real and very dangerous. And Dad wasn't allowed to communicate with us or tell us how long he'd be gone. Sometimes they lasted a few days, sometimes weeks. When I was in fourth grade, he'd gone on one that lasted almost two months.

And guess what I'd gotten on the last day of Hanukkah? I mean, besides a few mystery books and a bag of gelt (they're gold-wrapped chocolate coins). That's right: a video call from Dad with the news that he'd been assigned to another "training mission." He'd left the last week of February, and we hadn't heard from him since.

I kept my gaze on the timer. "No, it's not that! I told you, she just happened to be under the waffle iron. Speaking of, drumroll, please!" I lifted the lid with a flourish to reveal a perfect waffle. "Ta-da!"

"Beautiful," Mom said with a smile.

Grabbing a spatula, I gently lifted the waffle out and slid it onto a plate. Then I poured another ladleful of batter on the griddle and closed the lid. "Could you hand me the glaze?"

"Sure thing."

I busied myself icing the waffle. "So my coding group has a cool new project to do," I said, and I told Mom about the talent show and our voting feature for the talent show app.

"That sounds fun!" she said. "But isn't the talent show in a few weeks?"

"Next Friday! I can't *wait*." I paused, making a face. "Except you'll never guess what we found out today." Mom looked up at me expectantly. "Mrs. Clark is leaving. She got a job at TechTown."

"Oh no!" Mom put down her glass. "I'm sorry to hear that. I know how much you girls love her."

"Yeah." A memory of my not-quite panic attack flashed through my mind. I *did* love Mrs. Clark, but why had her news triggered that kind of reaction? I'd outgrown the whole panic-attack thing by the time I started middle school. My last therapist had said so herself.

"Earth to Erin . . . everything okay, hon?"

My head snapped up. "What? Yeah!" I handed the plate to Mom, along with a fork. She took a bite and closed her eyes.

"Omigod. Perfection."

I grinned. "Thanks." Turning back to the counter, I took my waffle out of the iron and started icing. No sooner had I finished when Mom cleared her throat.

"So this has nothing to do with Brave Bonnie Broomstick, but have you taken a look at that list of therapists I gave you?"

I swear, mothers are mind readers.

Sighing, I cut my waffle with my fork. "Some, yeah."

"Any you want me to call?" Mom asked carefully. "Just for a trial session?"

"Nah, not yet." I chewed my waffle and closed my eyes. It *was* good but not perfect. I made a mental note to adjust the cream-cheese-to-sugar ratio next time so the glaze wouldn't be so sweet.

"Maybe we can go over the list together tonight and

pick one or two to call first. What do you think?"

I took another bite, stalling for time. It wasn't that I didn't want to find a new therapist. My last one, Jillian, was amazing. Really funny, too.

And I *had* looked at Mom's list. She'd found a ton of therapists who all sounded great. But there were so many to choose from, it always ended up making me feel even more overwhelmed. Reading bios on their websites wasn't going to help me find a therapist I liked as much as Jillian.

"Can't—I've got a group-text date with my coding club group," I told Mom. "We need to brainstorm more about this voting feature."

"Ah, gotcha. After that, maybe?"

"I don't know, I have a ton of homework," I replied. "Literally, tons. I had to use a forklift just to get my backpack home."

Mom smiled, though her eyes still had that worried glint. "Erin, I really think it's important that we find a new therapist. Don't you agree?"

"I do," I said, and I meant it. "It's just not urgent. I don't get panic attacks anymore."

Mom arched an eyebrow. "Who said anything about panic attacks?"

Whoops.

I turned my attention back to my waffle. "I'm just saying, that's the reason I started therapy in the first place. But I haven't had a panic attack in years because I've learned how to manage them." Clearing my throat, I began ticking points off on my fingers. "First of all, I have film club, and extracurriculars are therapist-recommended to help manage anxiety. Second of all, now I have coding club, too. Twice the extracurriculars, twice the anxiety-managing powers! And third of all, Dad went on two training missions last year and how many panic attacks did I have? That's right: *zero*. Nada. Zilch."

"All fair points," Mom admitted. But I couldn't help noticing the way she kept glancing at Brave Bonnie Broomstick. And when I hugged her before heading off to my room, I could tell from the way she squeezed me extra hard that the therapy talk wasn't over.

It was like in coding, when a loop tells a program to perform an action over and over again while a condition is true.

```
while (dad_is_on_a_mission) {
worry_about_Erin( );
}
```

My mom was totally caught in that loop. I found myself wishing I could write code that would program her to stop worrying about me.

```
if (erin.panic_attacks == 0) {
mom.believe(erin);
}
```

I laughed to myself and made a mental note to tell my coding friends about my magic mom-programming code. Then I realized that would require telling them about Dad's mission and my panic attacks.

Mental note: deleted.

It's not like I was ashamed or anything. And I knew my friends would be supportive if I *did* tell them. But the panic attack thing wasn't a thing anymore. What happened today in coding club was just a tiny glitch. Nothing to see here, folks. Move along.

My phone started buzzing the second I walked into my room. I flopped down on my bed, setting Brave Bonnie Broomstick next to me.

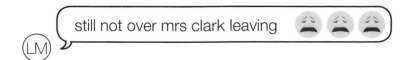

LM · still not over mrs clark leaving 😣 😣 😣

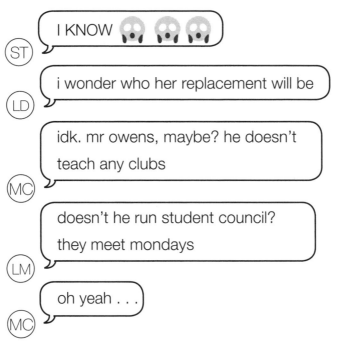

ST: I KNOW 💀 💀 💀

LD: i wonder who her replacement will be

MC: idk. mr owens, maybe? he doesn't teach any clubs

LM: doesn't he run student council? they meet mondays

MC: oh yeah . . .

I smiled, thumbs flying over my phone.

ER: replacement should be the prez of techtown. they take one of ours, we take one of theirs! #battlecry ✊

MC: lol!!

ST: hahaha

LM: seriously!! 👍 👍

24

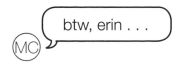

MC: btw, erin . . .

My stomach suddenly clenched. Had Maya noticed my not-quite panic attack during Mrs. Clark's announcement? We'd only been friends since I moved to town at the beginning of the school year, but Maya knew me pretty well. Especially considering how much time we spent hanging out because of coding club. I held my breath until her next text appeared.

MC: seriously, what's your talent show act gonna be??

I exhaled a huge sigh of relief, a grin spreading over my face as my friends chimed in with suggestions.

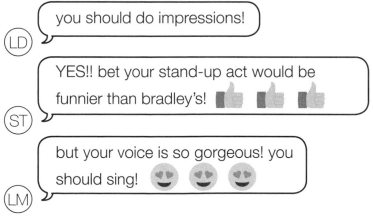

LD: you should do impressions!

ST: YES!! bet your stand-up act would be funnier than bradley's!

LM: but your voice is so gorgeous! you should sing!

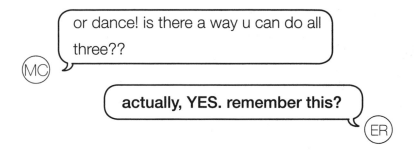

MC or dance! is there a way u can do all three??

ER actually, YES. remember this?

Quickly, I opened a web browser and searched for my favorite viral video of all time—it was of a little girl singing—then copied the link and pasted it into our group text. Half a minute later, my friends started to respond.

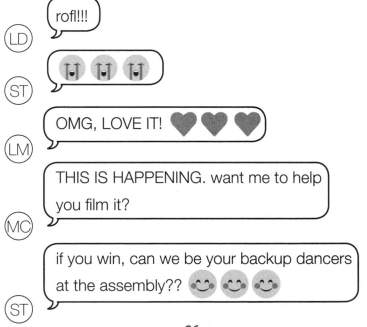

LD rofl!!!

ST 😭 😭 😭

LM OMG, LOVE IT! 🖤 🖤 🖤

MC THIS IS HAPPENING. want me to help you film it?

ST if you win, can we be your backup dancers at the assembly?? 😊 😊 😊

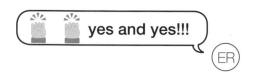
yes and yes!!!

ER

I was bouncing on my bed with excitement. The text conversation turned to voting-feature details and splitting up tasks, but I couldn't stop thinking about my talent show act. It would be a *lot* of work, between film club and coding club, especially considering I had already committed so much time for the talent show. But that was a good thing. And necessary.

All the Talents was going to be *All the Distractions* I needed until Dad's mission was over.

Chapter Three

By lunch the next day, Mrs. Clark had helped Bradley's group get the *All the Talents* web app up online. It was just a home page—no actual videos or features yet—but the whole school was buzzing about it. Maya and I passed by Bradley in the hot-lunch line as we headed to our table.

"Nice job getting the site up so fast!" Maya said. "Although it looks kinda plain..."

Bradley took a plate heaped with mashed potatoes and set it on his tray. "Oh, just you wait," he said with a grin. "We're working on a super-cool design. We just wanted to get something up online with the rules for entering so everyone can start making their videos."

I nodded. "Good call, since the first round's due Monday." My stomach did a flip as I said it. After our group text last night, it was pretty obvious the voting part was going to be really complicated to code. And while it was going to be fun, it probably wouldn't leave me with much time to film my audition.

"Why don't I come over Saturday afternoon?" Maya asked. "I can help you get set up and film."

"That'd be great!" I answered. Apparently best friends also had mind-reading powers.

In front of Bradley, a tall girl in a cute blue-plaid romper turned around. "Hey, Maya!" she said eagerly.

Maya smiled. "Hi, Hannah. Love your headband."

Hannah touched the wide purple cloth wrapped around her cropped black curls. It complemented her dark skin perfectly. "Thanks! Hey, I heard you're doing a fashion show for *All the Talents*, and—"

"What?!" I whirled around, staring at Maya. "Are you really? That's so cool!"

"Yeah," Maya said, toying with her long beaded necklace. "Designing is a talent, too. My video will be a fashion runway, with girls modeling my outfits."

"That's what I wanted to ask you about," said Hannah. "If you're looking for models, I'd love to do it! Your dresses are *amazing*."

"Sure!" Maya exclaimed, surprising me when her

voice shot up an octave. "You'd be a great model. I mean, because . . . um . . ."

I stared at her. Was Maya blushing? I'd never seen her so flustered.

"Because you're so tall," I finished for her, smiling at Hannah. "And because you've clearly mastered walking."

Hannah laughed. "Cool! I'll text you later about it, okay?"

Maya nodded, still pink faced. "Yeah, okay!"

We headed to our table, and I nudged her elbow. "What was that about?"

"What? Nothing," Maya said quickly. "Oh hey, don't let me forget to ask Sophia if I can use that dress I made her for the dance."

My heart warmed at the memory of Sophia walking into the winter school dance, all eyes on her. Maya had sewn all these lights into the fabric of Sophia's dress, and then programmed them to blink and flash to the music. It was amazing.

"So a fashion runway, huh?" I asked. "That's going to be *so* cool!"

Maya beamed. "Thanks! I'm really excited."

Lucy, Leila, and Sophia were already deep in

conversation when Maya and I sat down.

"I ran into Mrs. Clark right after third period," Lucy told us immediately. "She said a ton of students already signed up for the talent show. And enrollment is open until tomorrow!"

"Wow," I said, unwrapping my sandwich. "Film club's gonna be busy. We have to screen all the videos and approve them before they go up on the site."

Maya bit into a carrot stick with a loud crunch. "You know, most reality shows have a few rounds," she said thoughtfully. "Maybe we should consider that, since so many people are entering."

"I like that," Sophia said. "We could narrow down the contestants to a small group. It would make things more exciting, too!"

"Not to mention more work for everyone in coding club," I added.

Lucy tilted her head. "You don't think we should do it?"

"No, I think we *should!*" I exclaimed. "It definitely makes sense for the talent show." Then I stuck my arms straight out. "Work . . . need work . . . ," I droned in my best zombie voice.

Everyone laughed. Then Lucy leaned forward and grabbed my arm.

"If you really want more work, I have an idea."

"You want me to do your homework?" I pretended to consider it. "Okay. Twenty bucks per page."

"Ha ha." Smiling, Lucy sat up straighter. "That's not what I meant. I'm still bummed about Mrs. Clark leaving coding club, and this morning I asked Principal Stephens who was going to replace her. He said he's still working on it, but he has several teachers who are interested."

"Oh cool!" said Leila, and the rest of us nodded.

"Yeah, it is," Lucy responded. "But I started thinking, how is he going to choose the best one? They all have different qualities, kind of like the talent show contestants . . ."

She stirred her yogurt and looked at us, eyebrows raised. After a few seconds, Maya cleared her throat.

"And?"

Lucy sighed. "*And*, we're already working on a voting feature that narrows down contestants based on qualities, right? I bet once we finish, we could modify it to help pick the best coding club teacher!"

Sophia looked confused. "So everyone in coding club would vote for a new teacher? Couldn't we just do a headcount instead of using an app?"

"No, I mean we could use it to gather data," Lucy explained, gesturing with her spoon like she was gathering data out of the air. "For the talent show, everyone will give contestants thumbs-ups based on creativity, presentation, and all of those qualities, right? So we can choose qualities for an ideal coding club teacher, enter all the teachers Principal Stephens is considering, and then get as many students as possible to vote, so we'll have lots of data to help him choose the best one. I was going to ask him about it right after school today, as long as you're all in. You are, right?"

Her eyes were sparkling, but I could tell the other girls weren't nearly as excited. And I had to admit, while it was definitely a cool idea, it did seem like another big commitment on top of our already intense deadlines.

But until I heard from Dad, I was determined to keep myself distracted. Plus, I didn't want to disappoint Lucy. If theater was my one true love, coding was definitely hers—she'd been so passionate about it right from our very first meeting. Mrs. Clark leaving was probably harder on Lucy than it was on the rest of us. No wonder she was so eager to find a good replacement.

"Dahling, what an absolutely *brilliant* idea!" I exclaimed in a pompous British accent, pushing my glasses to the tip of my nose and peering over the frames. "Top drawer. Absolutely corking."

"It is a good idea," Sophia said, laughing along with the others. "But honestly, softball tryouts start next week, so between that and working on this voting feature for the app, I'm going to be pretty busy."

Maya nodded. "Same here. I'm entering the talent show, and—"

"You are?" Leila interjected, beaming. "Me too! I'm trying to program a robot to play a song on a toy xylophone. What are you doing?"

Maya told everyone about her fashion-runway idea, and soon the conversation had turned to Sophia's dress and all the other cool stuff Maya might design. I glanced over at Lucy. She had a funny, tight expression on her face.

"Erin, you're entering, too, right?" she asked me, and I nodded. "But you can still help me with this? I just want to make sure we get the best possible replacement for Mrs. Clark."

An awkward silence descended over the table. Maya and Sophia glanced at each other, and Leila stared down at the apple in her hand. My stomach tightened a little.

"I know!" I told Lucy, keeping my voice as upbeat as possible. "We all do."

"So you're in?"

"Of *course,* dahling," I answered, hoping to lighten the mood. But this time, no one laughed.

"Are you sure, Erin?" Maya asked, eyebrows arched. "You just said film club is going to be really busy, too."

"It's no biggie," I said airily, opening a carton of milk. "Actually, I figured out the trick to keeping up with everything—no sleep! It totally works, I swear. All you have to do is stay up all night and . . ." Trailing off, I thunked my head down onto the table and let out a loud snore. The sound of my friends' laughter sent a wave of relief through me, and my shoulders relaxed. "Just kidding," I continued, sitting up. "I'm giving up my favorite TV shows for the next few weeks to make time for this stuff, that's all."

Leila gasped. "So you didn't watch *Spyland* last night? The ending was amazing, they—"

"I can't hear you, lalala!" I plugged my ears with my fingers, and my friends started giggling.

The awkwardness finally seemed to be gone, thank

goodness. But as the conversation turned to our favorite shows, I felt a familiar and unwelcome flutter of anxiety in my chest. Maya was right—I had a *lot* of commitments over the next few weeks. Could I really keep up with them all?

That's the point, I told myself firmly. Every minute I spent working on something was a minute I wasn't worrying about Dad. *All the Distractions* was a stellar plan.

Chapter Four

Film club stayed an hour later than usual Wednesday after school, watching the videos students had submitted and approving them to go up online. It seemed like every time we finished one, two new ones popped up. It was awesome, but by the time I got home from school, my head was spinning. After dinner, I cast a longing look at the television before getting started on my homework.

By Thursday morning, over fifty kids had uploaded videos to the *All the Talents* app.

"The first round is going to be *huge*," Maya said, watching me twirl the combination on my locker. "I can't believe how fast everyone's making these videos."

"I know! It's so cool. How's yours coming?"

"Well, I figured out which five outfits I want to use

for the fashion show, but two of them aren't finished," Maya replied. "What about you? Have you practiced your act yet?"

"You mean besides every morning in the shower?" I slammed my locker closed, then held an imaginary microphone to my mouth and started to belt out a song. "*I know you don't think so*—oh no, my soap!" I grabbed and snatched at the air, like an invisible bar of soap kept slipping through my fingers, and Maya cracked up.

"I can't wait to see the real act," she said, her eyes glowing. "Are we still on for filming Saturday?"

"Yeah! Is noon okay?"

"Yup!"

My phone lit up with a text message from Lucy.

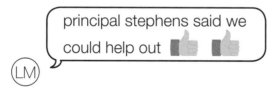

I quickly texted back.

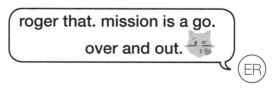

Maya gave me a look but I shook my head.

"My project with Lucy," I told her. "Finding a replacement for Mrs. Clark."

"Is that okay?" Maya asked. "I mean—"

Both our phones buzzed at the same time, cutting her off. This time, it was the group chat.

> can u guys make it to an extra coding
> club meeting after school today?
> mrs clark said she'll be there for
> anyone who needs more time on their
> projects

Maya sighed. "I really need to work on those outfits . . . I don't know." She glanced up at me. "Can you make it?"

"Definitely," I answered without hesitation. I hadn't been looking forward to going home to an empty apartment and no messages from Dad. "But don't feel bad if you can't go."

"Nah, I'll go, too." Maya was already typing a response. "We do have a lot to do on that program. Maybe your no-sleep idea isn't so bad after all."

"*Sleeeeeeeep,*" I moaned, sticking my arms straight out. Maya shrieked when I gnashed my teeth. She hurried down the corridor, looking over her shoulder and giggling as I zombie-stomped after her.

When I walked into Mrs. Clark's room after school, she and Lucy waved at me from behind Lucy's computer.

"I was just taking a look at what you girls have done so far on your feature for our site," Mrs. Clark told me. "I'm so impressed!"

Lucy half stood out of her chair, peering at the door. "Did you see Sophia or anyone else?" she asked with a frown.

I shook my head. "No. I'm sure they're on their way, though. So whaddaya say, kiddo?" I said in a nasal voice like an old-timey reporter, cracking my knuckles and wiggling my fingers. "Ready to start coding?"

Lucy laughed. "Ready!"

Mrs. Clark headed back to her desk as Lucy and I got to work. After a slow start—and a few questions for Mrs. Clark—we fell into a groove, coding the specifics for our voting system that we'd talked about the night before. But Lucy kept glancing at the door with an increasingly irritated expression, and the knot in my stomach kept getting tighter and tighter. Where *were* the others?

When Leila and Maya finally burst through the door, I exhaled a huge sigh of relief.

"Sorry I'm late," Leila said, pulling up a chair next to

Lucy. "Tania called—I needed to ask her a few questions about my robot before I work on it some more tonight."

Leila's older sister, Tania, was just as into robots and programming as Leila. She was also super smart and nice—I'd met her a few times. She was planning to go back to Pakistan (where they were from) after college and make robots that would help farmers.

"I'm sorry, too." Maya flopped down next to me. "I ran into Hannah and lost track of time. She has so many amazing ideas for her outfit!" Her cheeks were all pink again, just like at lunch.

"Like what?" I asked enthusiastically. "Did you take my suggestion to add wings that actually work?"

Maya laughed as I flapped my arms. "No wings, sorry. But it's going to be *almost* as cool."

I faked a disappointed pouty look. "I can't wait to see it," I said. But Lucy didn't say anything—she just kept typing. A second later, Sophia trudged into the classroom, wiping her sweaty face on her sleeve.

"Sorry, guys. I was at softball tryouts," she huffed.

"How were they?" I asked, and she beamed.

"Awesome," she replied, pulling out the chair next to Maya's. "I think the team's going to be amazing this year. We—"

"Here's what we've done so far," Lucy interrupted. She turned her monitor so Maya and Sophia could see the code we'd written. "But if we're going to get at least a draft of this finished by tomorrow, we need to split up the work."

"That's why we're here," Maya said tightly. Next to her, Sophia rolled her eyes.

I could feel the tension rising in our group. I had to do something.

"Speak for yourself!" I joked, wiping my suddenly sweaty palms on my jeans. "I'm here for these super-comfy chairs." I leaned back in the rolling chair until it started to tip over, then grabbed Lucy's arm. "Ack, help!"

To my relief, she finally cracked a smile. "They're not recliners, you goofball."

"Well maybe they *should* be," I said fervently. "Can you imagine how awesome class would be?"

"You'd just fall asleep!"

"Exactly—power naps." I closed my eyes and let out a loud, fake snore that made my friends giggle. Then I sat up straight and clapped my hands. "Wow, I feel *so* much better. Let's do this!"

Lucy looked a bit calmer, and so I relaxed, too. Tension

defused. After Lucy explained to the others what was left to do, everyone chose a task. For a few minutes, we wrote code in silence. Nice silence, though—not the awkward kind. It felt like good old coding club again.

"So what ideas did Hannah have for her dress?" I asked Maya, and her face lit up.

"Actually, they're about her accessories," she said excitedly, fingers still flying over her keyboard. "And fabrics. I started sketching a few ideas while we were talking, and they already look awesome. They're a bit more complicated than anything I've made before, but it'll be a great way to try some new materials and sewing techniques."

"You could really grow as a designer," I said. "You know, get to the next level. Really … spread your wings."

Maya faked a glare.

"I'm not designing wings," she said.

"The more you deny it … ," I said, with a shrug.

"Shut up." She finally cracked a smile. "No, Hannah had some really great ideas."

"Like what?" I asked.

Soon we were chatting about Maya's fashion show, then Sophia's softball tryouts, and then Leila's robot. We were making progress on the site, too, and I could tell even Lucy had started to relax. An hour later, Mrs. Clark was looking over a finished draft of our app.

"Great work," she told us, scrolling through pages of code. "Next step will be beta testing, which is usually the last stage before an app is released. We need someone outside of the club to try using all the features to check for problems. But before we do that, we should get one of you to test it for bugs before tomorrow." She glanced at the clock. "Whoops, I didn't realize how late it is! We'd better get going."

Mrs. Clark hurried back to her desk as the rest of us started putting on our jackets.

"So, testing for bugs," Leila said slowly. "Who wants to do it?"

I bit my lip. Part of me wanted to volunteer—work zombie and all that—but I had a history test tomorrow, and a ton of algebra homework, and more videos to sort through for film club. So I waited until someone else spoke up.

"I'd do it, but I really need to get started sewing," Maya finally responded.

Leila nodded. "Yeah, I wanted to spend tonight working on these fixes Tania suggested . . ."

I glanced at Sophia, who was slowly zipping up her

backpack. She looked exhausted from tryouts, and I knew she probably wanted to go home and crash.

Lucy sighed. "Well, I was going to work on the teacher app tonight. But if none of you can do it . . ."

"I can!" I blurted out, because that weird, awkward tension was back, and I couldn't stand it. "It's no problem."

"Cool!" Lucy beamed at me. "Thanks, Erin. Hey, maybe we can chat while we're working! I can show you what I've done with the teacher app so far."

"Sounds fun!" I smiled at Lucy, but I couldn't help noticing the expressions on my other friends' faces. A little bit irritated, a little bit uncomfortable. I fought down yet another wave of anxiety as we followed Mrs. Clark out of the classroom.

Was this just how things were going to be now? I knew everyone had a lot going on—myself included— but coding club had never been stressful before. I figured we'd be able to relax after the talent show, but then Mrs. Clark would be gone. Besides, we'd been under pressure before, like while trying to get our robot to dance at the hackathon, or figuring out how to incorporate coding into the future-themed winter dance. But even then, we'd had fun. What if coding club never went back to how it had been?

The second I got home, I made a beeline for the computer in the living room and opened a chat window. The little circle next to Dad's name was gray for offline. *The perfect color,* I thought glumly. Gray matched my mood exactly.

I left the window open while I did my algebra homework, then read a few chapters of my history textbook. By the time I finished, my eyes were ready to fall out of their sockets. But Mom would be home in half an hour, and I still had to test the voting part for bugs.

Ten minutes later, I could feel a headache starting to throb behind my temples. Our voting feature looked good, but I'd already hit a few problems trying it out. I'd created a fake talent show candidate, and I was experimenting with giving thumbs-ups on different combinations of all the qualities we'd entered. But no matter how many thumbs-ups I clicked, it just kept giving my fake candidate a "three" for her overall score. And when I clicked enter to submit my vote, the site wasn't saving the new vote to the database. I'd just started reading over our code to try and find the problem when a little flash of green in the chat window caught my eye.

Hope rushed through me, quickly followed by disappointment. The green light was next to Leila's name, not Dad's. Still, maybe Leila could help me figure out these bugs. I double-clicked her name, then started typing.

> **Erin**: LEILA!!! helllllllp this bug test is NOT going well and I'm stressing out big-time 😠 😠 😠

I waited, drumming my fingers on the desk. A few seconds later, a response popped up.

> **Leila:** hi, Erin! this is Tania—Leila must've forgotten to log out.
>
> **Erin:** oh! hi tania. plz ignore my message. 😬 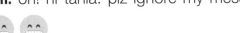 😬 😬

Sighing, I leaned back in my chair. Should I text Leila? Or anyone else from coding club? I knew they were all busy with other stuff tonight . . . but hey, I had a lot to do, too. Yet here I was, tackling our group project alone.

Because you volunteered, I reminded myself firmly. *Stop complaining.*

A loud beeping noise startled me, and I looked at the

screen. A little window had popped up.

Accept call from Leila Devi? **Yes/No**

I clicked yes, and a second later, Tania's face filled the screen.

"Hey!" she said. "Haven't seen you since spring break. Break any more hula-hooping records lately?"

I burst out laughing. "Oh, I forgot about that!" Over the break, Leila had us all over for a sleepover. Tania ended up judging our hula-hoop competition, which I won by a mile—twenty-four minutes, thank you very much. Hula-hooping was my secret talent. "No new records lately," I told her. "Had to give my hips a chance to recover."

"Gotcha." Tania grinned. "So what's up with the bug testing?"

"Oh!" I blinked, surprised. "It's okay, I can figure it out."

"Really?" Tania asked. "Because if you think another pair of eyes would help, I don't mind. I'm happy to help out my sister's friend."

"Well, okay," I admitted. "I'm not sure what's wrong. But you didn't have to call!"

Tania shrugged. "Leila told me coding club's been a little stressful this week." She glanced over her shoulder, and I caught a glimpse of a pretty flowery pattern on her scarf. "She's in the garage right now, working on her robot for the talent show. Anyway, if you really need help, I've got a few minutes!"

Since she was offering, I figured I might as well get her help. "That would be *awesome*." I sent her the link to the web app, along with a password and directions for navigating to the voting feature, and then started describing the problems I was having.

"Ah, I bet I know what's going on with the threes," Tania murmured, squinting at her screen. "Yup, right here. Instead of having the feature count the number of thumbs-ups, this code is instructing it to count numbers one, two, and three. That's why you keep getting threes!"

"Oh!" I found the code she was talking about. "Yeah, you're right. Well, that's probably an easy fix, right?"

"Yup!" Tania helped me adjust the code, and the next time I rated my fake candidate, it counted the number of thumbs perfectly.

"Success!" I cheered, and Tania laughed. "But, look, this is an even bigger problem." I clicked enter, and

Tania and I went into the dashboard. "No data," I said. "What's that about?"

Tania's brow furrowed. "Hmm, that is a bit trickier..."

We spent the next fifteen minutes poring over code. After a few wrong guesses, we finally identified the problem and ran a final test. Every time we reloaded the page, we accidentally reset the database. Tania helped me fix that bug, too. When the results showed up in the dashboard, I raised my arms in a V for victory, then slumped over in my chair like I'd passed out.

Tania was laughing again. "Hey, no more stressing!" she said. "I hope you can relax the rest of tonight?"

I shrugged. "Eh, I still have a little studying to do. Plus I should start preparing for my talent show video."

Her eyes widened. "You're entering the talent show, too? And Leila told me you're in film club ... wow, Erin. No wonder you're stressed!"

"The only stressful part was trying to decide between singing and hula-hooping," I joked, spreading my arms and wiggling in my chair as if I was practicing. "Thanks again for calling, by the way. I never would've finished this tonight without you."

"Anytime! Let me know if you need any more help, okay?"

"I will, thanks!"

I waved, then closed the screen. The circle next to Dad's name was still gray.

Anxiety fluttered through my stomach, and I ignored it. It was Thursday, which meant Mom would be picking up Chinese takeout for dinner. And thanks to my delicious stress-baking habit, we could have dessert tonight, too. If I hurried, I could get a batch of cupcakes in the oven before she got home.

Chapter Five

"*I know you don't think so, but it's tru-u-ue ...*"

I stepped back, studying the blue sheet I'd pinned on my bedroom wall. Not the most exciting backdrop for my talent show act, but I'd read online that it was best to keep it simple—that way the focus would be on my performance.

"*So stand back, look out, let me show you-ou-ou ...*"

On my laptop screen, a little girl in overalls clutched a stuffed monkey. She was singing a song she made up— and her voice was amazing. But that wasn't the reason her video had gone viral last summer. Nope, those hundreds of thousands of hits were all because of her dance routine, which was *hilarious*. It was like a cross between ballet and a short-circuiting robot, with a few random karate moves thrown in for good measure.

My dad had been in town then, and we'd watched it together, both of us laughing so hard tears were streaming down our faces. From then on, any time I wanted to make Dad smile, all I had to do was sing a few lines. He'd start cracking up before I even busted into the dance moves.

My old keyboard sat on my desk in front of the laptop, along with a little speaker. I'd stayed up way too late last night composing a piano accompaniment to the song. It was really simple, but I'd added a few sound effects to the recording. I had to admit, this performance had everything: singing, dancing, and comedy. All my talents combined.

I imagined myself standing onstage at the assembly, one of the top three finalists. The house lights would go down, and a spotlight would hit me. I'd bring the microphone to my lips, my voice echoing out of the auditorium's giant speakers . . . and then I'd ditch the mic and bust into the dance, and the whole school would *lose* it.

I really missed performing. This was going to be so fun.

"Erin! Maya's here!"

Quickly, I hit pause on the video, then hurried out of

my room. Maya was in the kitchen with my mom, who was pouring two glasses of milk.

Maya grinned at me. "Your mom said something about cupcakes, and I figured, hey, maybe a snack before we film wouldn't be a bad idea . . ."

"Good call!" I said cheerfully, grabbing the plastic container off the counter and setting it on the table. After that tense coding club meeting on Thursday, I'd baked two dozen cupcakes. Mom had taken some to work yesterday, but we still had a bunch left.

Maya leaned over when I pulled the lid off. "Ahhh, those look so good. What kind are they?"

"Snickerdoodle, with buttercream frosting and a caramel drizzle," I answered proudly. Mom groaned, rubbing her stomach.

"Be careful, they're addictive," she told Maya. "I think I've eaten at least three in the last forty-eight hours."

Maya giggled. "I'll take the risk!"

I watched Mom rummage through her purse, then grab her keys off the counter. "Are you leaving?"

"Yeah, quick grocery trip." Mom smiled at me. "Besides, it's probably better if I'm not here while you make your video. You don't need me laughing my head off in the background."

"True," I agreed, and she gave me a quick kiss on the forehead.

"Have fun, girls!"

"Bye!" I waved before turning back to Maya. "Thanks again for helping me with this. I know you're busy with your fashion show, too."

"It's no problem! And you'll never guess what I brought." Maya took another bite of her cupcake, then unzipped her backpack. A second later, she pulled out a stuffed monkey.

"Oh wow!" I exclaimed. "That looks just like the one from the video! Where'd you get it?"

"Sophia gave it to me!" Maya replied. "It's her sister's. She was going to give it to you at lunch yesterday, but since you weren't there, I told her I was coming over to your place today."

"This is *perfect*," I said, taking the monkey and swinging him around. "Actually, I'm glad I went to film club instead of lunch. I haven't told anyone—except you—all the secret details about my audition. If anyone else saw this, it would've ruined the surprise."

"Oooh, good point!" Maya popped the last bit of cupcake in her mouth. "How was film club?"

"Super busy." That was an understatement. Watching

all the videos was fun, but after a while they started blurring together. And I was positive tons of kids—like me—would be making their video this weekend, so there would be even more to review on Monday. "We're all caught up for now, though," I added, reaching for my glass of milk. "I can't wait to see yours. How's it coming?"

Maya's face lit up. "Actually, Hannah came over after school yesterday and helped a ton—we finished all five outfits."

"Wow!" I exclaimed. "Are you making the video tomorrow? Who are your other models?"

"Actually, just Hannah for now," Maya said, and I noticed that faint blush was back. "I couldn't find anyone else to model, and she's not entering the talent show, so she has the time."

"Well, when you get into round two and then become a finalist, I bet it'll be easy for you to get a bunch of volunteer models for the assembly." I crumpled up my napkin. "And then you'll start your own fashion line and become super famous. Chung's Closet! No—M. C. Fashion! Wait, that sounds like you're a rapper . . ."

Maya laughed. "I think I'd go with Made by Maya."

"*Perfect.* Made by Maya—soon to be worn by every celebrity and model in the world," I announced. Pausing,

I eyed Maya. "And Hannah, of course."

"Yeah . . ."

I licked the frosting from my fingers, watching Maya carefully. She was gazing down at the table with a goofy little smile. "She seems really cool," I added lightly. "Think you'll keep hanging out with her after the talent show?"

Maya fiddled with her bracelets. "I hope so—I mean, if she wants to. I think she does. But I haven't, um . . ." Her cheeks were tomato red now, and I couldn't help it. I started giggling. "What?" Maya said, but I could tell she was trying not to smile, too.

"You *like* her," I replied triumphantly. "I knew it!"

Maya buried her face in her hands. "Oh no. Is it that obvious? Does everybody know?"

"No! At least, I don't think so." I snapped the lid back on the container of cupcakes. "Soooo . . ."

"Soooo what?"

"Soooo are you going to ask her out?" I waggled my eyebrows.

Maya's eyes widened. "Like on a date?"

"Why not?"

"Because . . ." Maya hesitated. "I'd like to, yeah. But how would I even ask?"

"Like this: Hannah, want to see a movie with me this weekend?"

"Sure, but friends see movies together all the time," Maya pointed out. "Even if she said yes, how would I know if it's a date?"

I shrugged. "I don't know. But hey, if you don't ask her, you'll never find out!"

Maya smiled a little. "Yeah, you're right." She drained her glass of milk, then set it down on the table. "Okay! Should we make the video that's going to win the talent show?"

"Oh, I don't know about that!" I grabbed the stuffed monkey, then led the way down the hall to my room. "Honestly, I haven't even had time to practice it this week."

"But you said you've done it before, right?" Maya asked, closing my bedroom door behind her. "Seriously, your voice is amazing and the dance part is going to be *so* funny. I really think you'll be in the top three. Our whole coding group does—that way we can dance backup! It would be even funnier."

"Ha, it would be!" I answered, my heart doing a little flip at the thought. Making this video would be fun, and I loved this new talent show format. But if I didn't make the three finalists after two rounds of voting, I wouldn't have another chance to perform onstage until next year. And I really, *really* missed that rush.

"Do you want to do a practice run first?" Maya took my phone off the dresser and flopped onto my bed.

"Nah, I'm good." I stood in front of the blue sheet and did a few stretches. "I've done this *so* many times for my dad. It always cracks him up."

Maya looked up at me. "Actually, I'm kind of worried I'll screw this up by laughing while we're recording, like your mom said."

I wagged my finger at her. "No laughing allowed, Chung," I said sternly.

"I'll try." She scooted farther back on my bed to get more into the frame, then opened the app on my phone. "Ready?"

"Just a sec." Holding the monkey under my arm, I flipped my keyboard on and found the recording. "Okay, go!"

I hit play and hurried back to the sheet, and Maya held up my phone and started recording. When the opening chords sounded through the speaker, Maya clapped her hand over her mouth to stop herself from laughing.

I bit the inside of my cheeks and focused on keeping my expression solemn. That was a huge part of why the little girl's video was so funny—she looked so serious, and her voice was so beautiful, that when she started doing her jerky, flaily-armed dance with the stuffed monkey, it totally caught everyone off guard.

"I know you don't think so," I sang, looking straight at my phone. *"But it's tru-u-ue . . ."* Turning my head, I gazed into the stuffed monkey's plastic eyes. *"I can move, I can dance, better than you-u-u . . ."*

Maya's shoulders were shaking now, but she held my phone steady as I sang the rest of the verse. Performing always gave me an adrenaline rush, and my heart was pounding in my ears. I ignored it and tried to concentrate on the song.

The last time I'd done this whole routine was last summer. It was the day before my dad was going overseas again, and he was packing his bag when I put the video on. When it got to the dance, Dad abandoned his packing and joined me, flailing and jumping around until we collapsed on the floor, laughing so hard we cried.

It felt wrong to be dancing by myself.

When I glanced up to make sure Maya was still

filming, for a split second I was sure that it was my dad sitting there. A buzzing noise filled my ears, barely noticeable at first, but it got louder and louder until I couldn't hear the accompaniment anymore.

"So stand back . . ." My voice cracked, and I swallowed hard. But the buzzing wouldn't go away. *"Look out,"* I managed to choke out, and suddenly I couldn't breathe.

"Erin?"

Bright spots danced in my vision. Distantly, I heard wheezing, like someone in the next room was hyperventilating. But it wasn't someone else. It was me.

This was a panic attack. A real one.

I squeezed my eyes closed and tried to remember what my first therapist had told me back in third grade. *Don't think about anything but your breathing. Slow and steady.*

Gradually, my short, shallow gasps for air grew longer and steadier. I realized I was on my knees, my hands pressed into the carpet. And a voice was saying my name, sounding every bit as panicky as I felt. I kept my eyes shut until my pulse started to slow down. When I opened them, I saw Maya kneeling next to me, her face pale.

"Erin, are you okay?"

I nodded, not trusting myself to speak yet. Slowly, the rest of my room came back into focus. The monkey lay on the floor next to me, and I could see the little girl still paused mid-dance on my laptop screen. The last few chords of the accompaniment sounded through the speakers, and then there was nothing but silence.

Shaking a little, I started to stand, and Maya held my arm and helped me over to my bed. I sat down and grabbed Brave Bonnie Broomstick, hugging her to my chest. Maybe I should've been embarrassed about needing a stuffed animal for comfort, but I knew Maya wouldn't judge me.

Maya sat next to me, her expression a mix of worry and fear, but she didn't say anything. I took one last, deep breath.

"So much for doing it in one take, huh?" I tried to make my voice light. Maya shot me a serious look, and I sighed. "Sorry. It's just—that hasn't happened in a long time."

"What was it?" Maya's voice was unusually high, and I felt a twinge of guilt at having scared her so badly. "Are you sure you're okay?"

"I'm fine, I promise," I told her, trying to smile. "It was a panic attack. I used to get them sometimes, but it hasn't happened since third grade."

Maya's shoulders relaxed a little. "Oh. Okay." She hesitated, chewing her bottom lip. "Why, though? I mean, what caused it just now?"

I squeezed Brave Bonnie Broomstick tighter. Part of me wanted to tell Maya all about my dad's mission, my mom's long list of therapists, my *All the Distractions* plan. But another, bigger part of me was terrified that talking about all that stuff would just trigger another panic attack—or worse, make her think there was something wrong with me.

Before I could decide, I heard the front door open and close.

"My mom's back," I said, my chest tightening a little. "Don't tell her, okay?"

"What?" Maya blinked. "Why? Doesn't she know about your panic attacks?"

"Yeah, of course." I tossed Brave Bonnie Broomstick aside and got to my feet. "But this one doesn't count. I mean, it wasn't a real . . . Look, it's just better if she doesn't know, okay? Please, *please* don't say anything."

"Okay," Maya whispered, but she looked more worried than ever. "So, um. Do you want to try the song again, or maybe wait a few—"

"I'm not entering the talent show," I said abruptly, surprising us both. The moment the words were out of my mouth, I knew it was the right call. Picking this song was a huge mistake. I couldn't get through it without thinking about my dad. And what if Maya was right, and I *did* make it into the top three? I loved performing more than anything, but what if this happened again? I imagined myself having a panic attack onstage in front of the whole school and suppressed a shudder. Totally not worth the risk.

Maya's mouth had fallen open. "What? Why not?"

"I'm so sorry, I can't believe I wasted your Saturday afternoon," I babbled as I closed my laptop and turned off the keyboard. "But I think between coding club and film club, I just—I'm too busy. It's totally fine!" I added when Maya started to protest. "Thanks for coming over. I really appreciate it."

"Okay . . ." Slowly, Maya headed for my door. "Erin, are you sure you're okay?"

"Yup, absolutely." I gave her a big, forced smile. "Hey, good luck filming your video tomorrow! And let me know if I can help!"

"Yeah, okay. Thanks."

Out in the hall, I could hear Mom putting away

groceries in the kitchen. I hurried to the front door with Maya, hoping Mom wouldn't hear. One look at the expression on Maya's face, and my mom would know something was up.

"Thanks again," I said, giving Maya a quick hug.

"Of course." She gave me a last concerned look, then left.

As soon as I closed the door behind her, I took another deep, slow breath. Then I plastered a smile on my face and went to help my mom unpack the rest of the groceries.

Chapter Six

I spent Sunday afternoon running more tests for bugs on our feature of the talent show app, writing an essay for English class, and worrying about seeing Maya at school. I thought I'd done a pretty good job convincing Mom that backing out of the talent show was a responsible decision based on all my other commitments, not a spontaneous freak-out due to picking a song that made me think of Dad.

Maya had been a witness to the freak-out, though. She'd promised not to say anything to Mom, but would she tell the others? I couldn't stop imagining a secret group text going on behind my back. I must have picked up my phone and started typing in our chat at least a hundred times by Sunday night, but I didn't actually want to talk about this over text. And while I didn't want to talk about it at school, either, that was my only other option. So by the time I got to lunch Monday, I'd made up my mind: If Maya hadn't already said anything, I was going to tell my friends everything.

Probably.

My stomach twinged with nerves as I spotted Maya, Lucy, Sophia, and Leila at our usual table in the middle of the cafeteria. What if I started talking about my dad and had a panic attack right there in front of half the school? I pushed that image from my mind and slid onto the bench next to Leila.

"Erin, check it out!" she said excitedly, holding her phone where I could see it. On the screen, a boxy little robot on wheels rolled up to a toy xylophone. A mallet was attached to the center of the robot, and as I watched, it started to hammer out a familiar melody.

"Mary had a li-ttle lamb...," I sang along, scrunching up my face and headbanging like a rock star, and Leila cracked up. "Seriously, that's so awesome!"

"Thanks," Leila said. "I think I'm going to keep working on it after the talent show. Maybe program it to play a more complicated song. I know it's probably not as cool as a lot of the videos film club is getting."

"Do you know how many more videos came in?" Lucy asked me.

"So many, we literally broke the entire Internet," I deadpanned, and she giggled. "But the good news is, I think our voting part of the *All the Talents* app is ready to go. I tested it a bunch all weekend. And your sister helped!" I added, nudging Leila's elbow.

"Yeah, she told me," Leila replied. "Thanks so much for doing that, Erin. I know you were busy making your video, too."

Sophia stifled a yawn. "Oh, that's right!" she said, looking from me to Maya. "How'd it go? Can we see it?"

Maya and I glanced at each other, and she bit her lip and looked down at her sandwich. Okay, so she hadn't told them what happened at all. Which meant it was up to me. My heart started pounding, and a fresh wave of anxiety flooded through me.

Nope. Not now.

"Actually, I decided not to enter," I said breezily, opening a bag of chips. "Too busy with other stuff, you know? Work zombie didn't have the brains to think ahead, ha ha."

Lucy and Leila looked surprised, but Sophia nodded.

"I totally get it," she said. "I spent the whole weekend

doing homework and helping out with chores. And every day after school I've either got coding club or softball tryouts. I never would've found time to make a talent show video, too!"

Lucy was still watching me. "Maybe you could take a day off from film club to make your video. I'm sure your teacher would understand."

I shrugged. "Eh, it's fine. Watching everyone else's videos is way more fun, anyway."

"But you're such a great performer! If you—"

"I don't want to." The words came out way louder than I'd intended, and I could feel Maya staring at me. Whoops. I put on a silly vampire accent. "Eh-vary-body is treated to entertainment by ze Great Erin Roberts eh-vary day. Vy not give others a chance to vin?"

My friends cracked up, and my shoulders slumped in relief.

"Besides," I added lightly, my voice back to normal. "I've never been a part of all this behind-the-scenes stuff for a show. It's cool!"

"It is." Leila smiled at me. "But I still think you would've won."

"Me too," Sophia added. "And I'm *really* sad we never got to see you do that dance."

"Or be your backup dancers," Lucy added. "Onstage, in front of the whole school . . . on second thought, maybe I'm glad you changed your mind."

Everyone laughed, and I could feel my anxiety draining away. I felt bad for not being completely honest, but a crowded cafeteria wasn't the best place for a serious talk, anyway. I'd tell my friends the truth later.

"So I finished the teacher app," Lucy told us. "Could any of you test it out?"

And suddenly, it was the bug-testing ordeal all over again. I could tell from the other girls' faces that no one wanted to volunteer—especially considering they'd already told Lucy they were too busy to help with the voting feature for the *All the Talents* web app. And honestly, the idea of doing even more testing for bugs after I'd done so much for the voting part on the site kind of made my head hurt. But the silence was getting awkward, and I didn't want Lucy to get upset. So I bounced up and down in my seat and waved my hand in the air.

"Oooh, pick me, pick me!"

Smiling, Lucy crumpled up her napkin. "Thanks, Erin! Ugh, I can't believe it's Mrs. Clark's last week teaching."

"It's going to be so weird without her." Leila sighed. "But I bet she'll love TechTown. Tania is actually trying to get an internship there."

Lucy's eyes widened. "Really? That's so cool! What would she be doing?"

As Leila told us more about the internship, I nodded along with everyone else. But now that I'd told my friends about backing out of the talent show, it was official, and the disappointment was sinking in. There was no chance I'd get to do my act onstage. Not that I cared that much about winning, but hey, maybe I *would've* had a shot.

My phone buzzed, and I glanced down to see a text from Maya.

She gave me a questioning look, and I smiled brightly at her before replying:

I slid my phone into my pocket and turned my attention back to Leila. But I couldn't help noticing

Maya giving me nervous glances for the rest of lunch. I wished I could find a way to reassure her that she had nothing to worry about. Plan *All the Distractions* was still totally working. I had made it through my history test, a practice timed essay in English, and a pop quiz in social studies without even a hint of a panic attack.

By the time I walked into Mrs. Clark's classroom for coding club, I'd forgotton about Maya's nervous looks and was in a pretty good mood.

"What's that?" I asked as I passed Bradley's computer. Then I stopped. "Whoa—is that the site?"

"Told you we were making some improvements," Bradley said with a snort. I had to admit, the design was *really* cool. The background was an image of our school, but with a blurry, pastel effect that made it look like a watercolor painting. *All the Talents!* stretched across the top, and below was a transparent box with information about submitting and another one with voting instructions.

Maddie reached over and grabbed Bradley's mouse. "Wait, you haven't seen the best part," she told me, scrolling down. Below the voting instructions was a collage of photos. Familiar photos. I leaned closer to the screen, my eyes widening.

"Are these screenshots?"

Bradley nodded. "All the ones that the film club has approved so far. There's mine!" He pointed to the photo of himself making a goofy face, and I grinned, remembering his stand-up act. It *was* pretty hilarious, I had to admit. And there was Leila's robot, and a picture from this amazing Claymation video Sarah Rodriguez had made, and Kyle Ward in the middle of a dance move . . .

Clutching my heart, I swooned and fell to my knees. "Guys, I am dead," I told them. "I am dead from the awesomeness of this site."

Maddie giggled. "Yeah, it was a lot of work. But we thought if everyone could see all the different kinds of acts that contestants were doing, maybe it would encourage even more people to enter."

"No problem there," I said. "I think at least half the school's submitted a video by now."

Lucy had the site open on her computer, too. Just like last week, she and I were the only ones in our group. I sat down next to her, and she sighed.

"Sophia's not coming," she told me. "Softball tryouts. I'm not sure where Maya or Leila are, though."

"I bet they'll be here soon." I tried to keep my voice

upbeat. And sure enough, Maya and Leila hurried into the room just as I finished logging into my computer. Maya turned to wave at someone in the hall, and I caught a peek of Hannah waving back right before the door closed.

Maya sat on my other side, and I nudged her with my elbow. "Did you talk to her?" I whispered, and she looked confused.

"Who?" Then she glanced at the door. "Oh, Hannah. No, not yet. I will, though!"

She gave me a weird, tight smile, then faced her computer. And just like that, my anxiety was back, a tiny knot in my stomach twisting more and more every second. Maya was definitely acting strange. Was it because she was nervous about asking Hannah out? Why wouldn't she just talk to me about it, like she did on Saturday?

Maybe it wasn't about Hannah at all. Maybe she was still weirded out about what happened over the weekend. For the next hour while we worked on adding our voting-feature code to the web app, Maya's eyes kept darting over to me, like I might start hyperventilating any second. And when Leila successfully voted on the first video with the whole club gathered around her computer, Maya was the only one who didn't cheer.

"We still have a lot to do this week," Mrs. Clark reminded us as we put on our coats and turned off our computers. "We'll need to monitor everything as students start to vote tomorrow, and be ready to address any bugs. But you all have done an *amazing* job with this site. I'm so impressed!"

The second we walked out of her classroom, I threw my arms up in the air. *"We are the champions,"* I sang, my voice echoing down the empty corridor.

"We kind of are," Leila agreed, pumping her fists.

"Remember the first day of coding club, with the peanut butter and jelly sandwiches?" I asked. "And now we can design a whole site in, like, a week!"

Lucy gave a sweeping look at all of us. "We are definitely the coding champions."

Everyone was in high spirits as we left the school. But as soon as I waved goodbye to my friends, the anxiety knot doubled in size. Because I knew I would check to see if Dad was online the moment I got home, and I was dreading seeing that little gray dot showing that he wasn't there.

I ducked my head against the chilly wind and tried to think about anything else. Like Maya. Maybe I should call her tonight so we could talk about Saturday. The more I thought about it, the better it sounded. I'd tell her all about my dad's mission and the panic attacks. And then I'd tell Lucy, Sophia, and Leila, too. Maybe it would even help get rid of the weird tension in our group once and for all.

By the time I was unlocking the front door, I felt better. But then I saw Mom sitting on the couch, and the expression on her face made my knees go rubbery.

"What's wrong?" I said immediately, my chest so tight I could barely breathe. "Is it Dad?"

Mom's eyes widened. "No, honey, he's—I haven't heard from him. I'm sure he's still fine."

I exhaled, my hands shaking. "Okay. But why are you home early?"

"Because Mrs. Chung called me during lunch." Mom looked at me with a mix of hurt and disappointment. "Erin, why didn't you tell me you had a panic attack this weekend?"

Chapter Seven

My relief that this wasn't about Dad was quickly replaced with dread. Maya's mom had told Mom about my panic attack . . . which meant Maya had told *her*. Now I knew why she'd been acting so weird all day. She hadn't been worried about me having another panic attack—she was worried about me finding out she'd told her mom about it.

"Um." My brain felt jammed. There was no point in denying anything, and I wasn't trying to think of a lie. I just didn't know what to say.

Mom was watching me silently. I took my time hanging up my coat in the front closet, then walked into the living room.

"I'm sorry," I said finally. "I didn't want you to worry. It wasn't a big deal."

"Erin . . ." Mom paused, and my throat tightened, because she looked more hurt than angry. She patted the empty space next to her on the couch, and I sat down. "You used to talk to me about your anxiety. You always told me about your panic attacks, and we handled them together. We were a team."

I swallowed hard. "I know, but . . . but this isn't like back then."

"It's not? How?"

"It's . . ." I shook my head. "I can handle it now. I've got distractions."

Mom's forehead wrinkled. "Distractions?"

"Yeah, remember? Jillian said theater was a great way to manage my anxiety," I said eagerly. "And now I've got film club *and* coding club to help me not think about . . . about . . ."

After a few seconds, understanding dawned on Mom's face.

"About your dad?"

I nodded, not trusting myself to speak.

"Erin, I do remember what Jillian said about theater," Mom said slowly. "But I don't think she meant it was good for you because it distracted you from important things. Overworking yourself isn't going to help you manage your anxiety—it might even make it worse."

"I'm not overworking myself!" I exclaimed.

"No? Then why did you drop out of the talent show? Because you told me it was that you'd taken on too much."

I had no response to that—she was totally right. But I couldn't tell her the truth. I couldn't tell her that just singing a song that reminded me of Dad had triggered my panic attack. It made me feel like a baby. I was older now; I should be able to handle his missions. So I just sat there, staring at the carpet.

"Sweetheart, I'm worried about you," Mom said softly. "I think maybe you need to take a break from your clubs."

"What?" My head snapped up. "No! That'll make things worse. Extracurriculars *help* anxiety! All my therapists said so!"

Mom sighed. "Erin, if you value therapy so much, why have you been putting off letting me call the therapists on the list I gave you?"

"Because I don't need one!" I said, frustration boiling over. "I needed one in elementary school, but I'm better now. I can handle this. And I don't have time for appointments after school, anyway." I stared down at the carpet again, not sure what to do with my hands.

"Actually, you do have the time." Mom's mouth was a thin line. "You dropped out of the talent show and lied to me about the reason why. You had a panic attack and didn't tell me about it. You're not being honest with me, and you're taking on way too much, which is not healthy. So until we get this sorted out, I want you to come home right after school every day."

"No, I can't!" I yelled. "We've got too much to do with the talent show this week, I have to—"

"I'll talk to your teachers," Mom interrupted. "I'm sure they'll understand."

"*You* don't understand," I snapped. "Dad would never make me quit my clubs."

I closed my mouth, surprised at myself. I'd never spoken to Mom like that before. She looked shocked, and even more hurt than before, but I swallowed my guilt.

"This conversation is over, Erin," she said quietly.

"Fine." I stormed off to my room. As soon as I slammed my door, tears welled up in my eyes. I flopped down onto my bed and instinctively grabbed Brave Bonnie Broomstick. Then I blinked, staring down at her fuzzy face and crooked buttons. Really? I still needed the same comfort toy I used in third grade?

"Nope," I announced, setting her back against my pillows. "Sorry, Bonnie. I can handle this on my own."

I pulled out my phone instead, opening the group text with my friends. My fingers hovered over the screen, and I glanced at the date on the last text in the chain. We hadn't texted since Friday because everyone was so busy.

My eyes grew hot again, but right before tears spilled over, my phone vibrated in my hands. I blinked down at the screen to see a string of text messages from Maya.

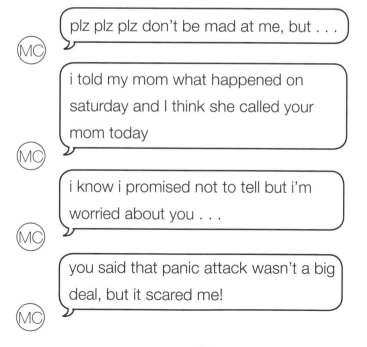

plz plz plz don't be mad at me, but . . .

MC

i told my mom what happened on saturday and I think she called your mom today

MC

i know i promised not to tell but i'm worried about you . . .

MC

you said that panic attack wasn't a big deal, but it scared me!

MC

The knot in my stomach loosened. My fingers shook as I typed my response.

I let out a shaky giggle, reaching for a tissue right as her next text popped up.

I blew my nose, threw the tissue in the trash can next to my bed, then took a deep breath.

yeah, since third grade when my dad started getting sent on these military missions. i never know how long it'll be till he calls again, and i get really worried about him. i was in therapy and it helped a lot. this is the first time I've had a panic attack since elementary school

ER

your dad's on a mission now?

MC

yeah, he left a few weeks ago 😟

ER

I hesitated, unsure of what else to say. Then I saw Maya was already responding.

erin, that SUCKS. 😢 😢 😢

MC

why didn't you say something before??

MC

> i was afraid even just talking about it would give me a panic attack!

ER

> that's why i had one on saturday. that song reminds me of my dad b/c i used to sing it for him all the time.

ER

> noooooooooooooo

MC

> i'm so sorry

MC

I felt about a billion times lighter reading Maya's texts. My thumbs flew over the screen as I sat on the edge of my bed.

> thx

ER

> so mom thinks i'm overworking myself and she's making me come home after school every day

ER

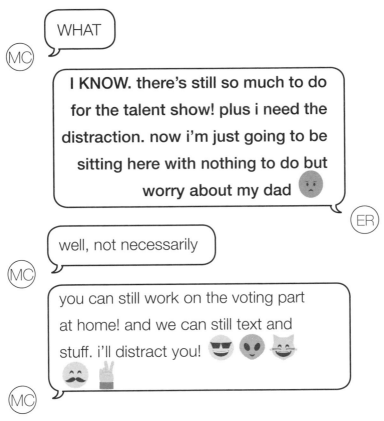

I sprawled out on my bed, tucking Brave Bonnie Broomstick under my head as a pillow. Maya was totally right. Being grounded didn't mean Plan *All the Distractions* was over. It just needed a little readjustment.

Chapter Eight

"Maya! Hey, Maya!"

Maya and I stopped right outside the entrance to the cafeteria, turning to see Hannah hurrying down the hall. She smiled at me before grabbing Maya's arm and shaking it excitedly.

"I was just in the computer lab checking the *All the Talents* site, and *guess what*," Hannah said.

"What?" Maya's cheeks were already pink, and I fought back a grin.

"Your video is ranked *second*!" Hannah exclaimed.

"Oh my god, seriously?" I yelped.

Maya looked stunned. "Really? Out of . . . everyone?"

"Out of every single audition," Hannah confirmed, her smile widening. "And I know voting for the first round is still open, but I really, *really* think you're going to be in the top three. Which means . . ."

She gave Maya an expectant look, and after a few seconds, Maya averted her gaze.

"Oh. That."

"What?" I asked, looking back and forth between them. Hannah bounced up and down on her toes.

"Maya's been working on something special," she told me eagerly. "For if—I mean, *when*—she's in the top three and gets to do her fashion show at the assembly."

"Ooooh, like a new dress or something?" I asked.

Maya nodded. "Yeah, I'm actually working on a bunch of new stuff . . . although Hannah can only model one on Friday, obviously. I mean, if I'm in the top three."

"You will be," Hannah and I said at the same time, and Maya laughed.

"You're the best. Both of you."

"We're also right," Hannah told her. "Which is why I just got permission from Ms. Davies to use the theater club's costume room during lunch! Want to go work on the outfits?"

"Right now?" Maya stared at her, then at me.

"Um, the answer is *yes*," I said, nudging her with my elbow. "Go!"

"Are you sure?" Maya gave me a meaningful look,

and I knew she was worried about her promise to distract me.

"Yes," I said firmly, giving her a confident smile. After a moment, Maya smiled back.

"Okay. Thanks, Erin."

She and Hannah hurried off down the hall, and I noticed Hannah was still clinging to her arm. Smiling to myself, I headed into the cafeteria.

Lucy and Leila were already at our usual table. So was Sophia, although I didn't notice her at first. Probably because she had her head on her arms like she was fast asleep. I sat next to her and gingerly poked her arm. When her eyelids fluttered open, I gasped.

"It's *aliiiive!*"

Leila gave me a gleeful look, but Lucy didn't even glance up from her social studies textbook. Sophia half-heartedly swatted at my hand.

"So sleepy," she mumbled. "I got to school an entire *hour* early today just to practice."

"Whoa," I said, unwrapping my sandwich. "Now that's dedication."

Sophia sat up and sighed. "Yeah. A few other girls trying out for pitcher are *really* good. I need all the practice I can get."

"I'm sure you'll kick butt," I told her, and she smiled gratefully.

"Hopefully. But I feel bad about missing coding club again, especially with the talent show this week. I hope you all don't mind."

Leila cringed. "Actually, I won't be there today, either."

"What?" Lucy finally looked up from her book, staring at Leila. "Why not?"

"It's the only day this week my sister has free," Leila explained. "And I need help on my robot. We just found out TechTown is having a robotics competition next week, and . . ." Leila paused, smiling bashfully. "Well, Tania thinks my robot is really good, and she talked me into entering."

"Whoa, that's so cool!" Sophia exclaimed, and I nodded eagerly.

"Awesome," Lucy said. "We'll miss you after school, though. Guess it'll be just us, right, Erin?"

Now it was my turn to cringe. "Actually . . ."

Lucy's smile vanished. "You're not coming, either?"

"I'm kind of grounded," I said, and her eyes widened. "For the rest of the week. So no coding club, no film club. Yay for me, right?"

"Oh no," said Leila. "What happened?"

I took a long sip of milk, suddenly wishing Maya was there. "It's a long story," I said finally, setting down the milk carton. "I had a fight with my mom because she thinks I'm overworking myself." I sat rigidly straight, letting my eyes go out of focus. "Work zombie . . . starving . . . ," I moaned, and they laughed. "But I can still work on the voting part for the site at home, Lucy," I went on in my normal voice. "Actually, maybe we can text while you're at coding club today! Keep me updated, and let me know if I can help with anything, okay?"

Lucy had a funny look on her face. "Yeah, okay."

And there it was: yet another awkward silence. I toyed with the straw in my milk carton, trying desperately to think of a joke or something to lighten the mood. But instead, anxiety crept into my chest, and I focused on breathing slowly. Inhale, exhale. Were my friends staring at me? Could they tell something was wrong? My pulse quickened, and I jumped when Sophia broke the silence.

"What's wrong?"

I opened my mouth, unsure of what to say. Then I realized she was staring at Lucy.

"Nothing," Lucy said, already turning her attention

back to her social studies textbook. But she looked up when Leila placed a hand on her elbow.

"It just seems like you've been upset for a few days now," she said softly. "Like when we were late to coding club last week."

"But we all worked really hard on the voting thing," Sophia added immediately. "It's not like we left you to do it by yourself."

"I know." Lucy finally closed her textbook. "That's not it. I guess I'm upset because I was up late last night working on the program to help us find a new coding club teacher."

I glanced at Sophia, who was staring at Lucy in disbelief. "Wait," she said slowly. "*That's* why you're mad at us? But that's *your* project!"

My heart started pounding in my ears, and I clasped my sweaty hands in my lap. *Stop,* I told myself. *Stop this. Calm down. Don't do this in the middle of the cafeteria.*

Lucy blinked in surprise. "It was my idea, but I thought we were all working on it together. And Principal Stephens said he'd look at the data I collect. Don't you care about finding the best teacher?"

"Of course we do," said Sophia. "But I told you I had softball tryouts. And Leila, Maya, and Erin were all entering the talent show, plus Erin had film club. We *told* you."

Lucy crossed her arms. "I know you're all super busy, but . . . I don't know. Coding club is important to me, and I thought it was to you, too."

"It is!" Sophia cried, and I closed my eyes. *Breathe in. Breathe out.* "But we already have so much going on. I mean, Erin's mom *grounded* her for overworking herself!" She gestured at me, then did a double take. "Erin? You okay?"

My breath was coming in short, sharp bursts. I could feel my friends watching me, and my throat started to feel tight.

"I have to go." I stood up so fast, I almost knocked over my milk carton. "See you all later." Before anyone could respond, I grabbed my bag and hurried off. I thought I heard someone call my name, but I bolted from the cafeteria without looking back.

Chapter Nine

The floor of the girls' restroom had exactly sixty-four square tiles, and seven were cracked. That was the kind of important information you learned after spending most of your lunch period hiding from friends, teachers, and basically all human beings. I'd been sitting on the floor next to the sinks for almost fifteen minutes, and no one had come in. Which was good, because I was feeling more like myself again. But it also made me feel bad. Had my friends tried to look for me at all? Or were they mad at me?

Standing, I tossed my empty lunch bag into the trash, then washed my hands. *Three more classes,* I told myself. *You can do it.* It dawned on me that I was grateful Mom was making me come right home after school.

I still had a few minutes until the bell would ring, but I wanted to get to class before everyone left the cafeteria. I hurried through the quiet halls, glancing into Mrs. Clark's room out of habit when I passed by. Then I did an abrupt about-face and looked again.

"Tania!"

Tania was behind Mrs. Clark's desk, squinting at her computer screen. She glanced up and gave me a warm look.

"Erin! How are you?"

"Fine," I said, stepping inside. "What are you doing here?"

"Mrs. Clark has been helping me with my internship application for TechTown," Tania explained. "She has her conference period after lunch, so I was just hanging out here until she gets back." She pointed to the screen, and I saw the *All the Talents* site. "Leila showed me this last night—looks like coding club did an awesome job!"

"It was so fun," I said, grinning. "Thanks again for helping me test the voting feature."

"Anytime," Tania said. "Stress levels back down to normal?"

I was startled for a moment, then remembered our conversation the other day. "Oh yeah. I'm . . . yeah."

Tania arched an eyebrow. "Not your most convincing performance, Miss Theater."

I laughed, but even I could hear how strained it sounded. "I'm fine, really. Just kind of grounded," I told her, surprising myself. But now the words were spilling out, and I couldn't seem to stop them. "And I dropped out of the talent show. And my friends might be mad at me. And my mom is *definitely* mad at me. And my . . ." My throat closed up, and I took a deep breath.

Tania was watching me closely, her brows knitted. "You've got a lot going on, huh?" I nodded, and she gave me a sympathetic smile. "I've been there. Last year, I got so stressed out the week of finals, I ended up hyperventilating in the middle of my calculus exam."

I stared at her. "Wait, seriously?"

"Yup." Tania nodded. "I was so embarrassed. Luckily, my teacher was great about it. She let me come after school to finish the test."

"Wow." I was surprised because that sounded a whole lot like a panic attack. And Tania was in high school! *And* she was super smart and cool. I had a hard time imagining her freaking out in the middle of class. But weirdly, knowing that she had made me feel a little bit better about myself.

My gaze wandered to the screen, and I noticed the thumbs-up buttons beneath all the videos. "Oh, I just realized I totally forgot to actually *vote*!" I exclaimed. "Earth to Erin. I can't believe I helped design the voting part of the site *and* watched all the videos during film club, and I haven't actually voted yet."

Tania stood and gestured at Mrs. Clark's computer. "Want to do it now, since it's already pulled up?"

"Sure, thanks!"

Quickly, I logged into the web app with my student ID. Then I used the search filter to find Leila's video. I clicked play, and her robot began to hit the toy xylophone, pinging out the familiar opening of "Mary Had a Little Lamb." Tania smiled as I started giving thumbs-ups to the qualities listed under her video.

"Leila's already made a ton of improvements since we filmed this," Tania told me. "I think she's going to do great in that robotics competition—did she tell you about that?"

"Yeah, just now at lunch!" I said, already moving over to Maya's video. "That is *so* cool."

Tania was quiet as I entered my ratings for Maya. When I finished, she cleared her throat.

"Speaking of lunch, why aren't you there now?"

"Um." I kept my eyes on the screen. "I left early."

"How come?"

"Well, we all kind of had a . . ." I paused. "Not a fight, exactly. But things are weird. And I had to leave the cafeteria because there were too many people around, and I was afraid I'd . . ."

I stopped and shook my head. Tania placed a hand on my arm.

"Afraid you'd what?" she asked gently.

"I was afraid I'd . . . I'd have a panic attack," I finished. "Because I had one last weekend, and I don't want it to happen again. Especially not at school."

I sank down in Mrs. Clark's chair, and after a moment, Tania sat on the edge of her desk.

"I get it," she said, smiling kindly. "I've been there. And like I said, I was totally embarrassed. But it turned out I didn't have to be. You know why?"

"Why?"

"Because my friends were so supportive," Tania said. "My teacher, too. Once I told them about my anxiety, they were so, so nice about it. And that meant I had one less thing to worry about."

I nodded, not trusting myself to speak.

"Have you told your friends?" Tania asked.

"Just Maya," I said, my voice thick. "I thought I could handle it by distracting myself with coding club and the talent show. That's what my old therapist said. I thought I was better, and the panic attacks were just because when I was little I couldn't handle anxiety."

Tania tilted her head. "Erin, anxiety has nothing to do with age. Adults can have anxiety, too. And it doesn't mean they can't handle things, or that they're immature. It's not necessarily something you grow out of. It's just something you learn to manage."

I pictured Brave Bonnie Broomstick lying on my bed and wiped my eyes. When the bell rang, I stood up. "Thanks for listening," I told Tania.

"Of course." She paused, then added, "Hey, Erin?"

"Yeah?"

"I think it's really cool that you talked to a therapist about this." Tania smiled at me. "Getting professional help was definitely the mature way to handle it."

I returned the smile, and the knot in my chest loosened a little. "Thanks, Tania."

She waved as I left Mrs. Clark's room. The halls were crowded by then, but I felt a million times calmer than I had in the cafeteria. Tania was right—my old therapist really did help me a lot. Finding a new one might be difficult, but I was ready to try.

First, there was someone else I needed to talk to.

I thought about what Tania had said all through my afternoon classes. On the walk home, I rehearsed exactly what I was going to say to Mom. I was sort of terrible at apologizing. Not because I had a hard time admitting when I was wrong, but I'd usually end up cracking a joke to make it feel less awkward. And according to Mom, that made whomever I was apologizing to feel like I wasn't taking it seriously.

I got to the apartment, dropped my backpack by the door, and hurried over to the computer. A gray dot next to Dad's name, as I expected. I wasn't sure why I even bothered looking anymore. Sighing, I sat down and started to type in the URL for the *All the Talents* site. Then I stopped, drumming my fingers on the desk. After a few seconds, I opened a search engine and started typing.

An hour later, the sound of the lock turning made me jump. I spun around in my chair as Mom walked in, then glanced at the clock on the computer screen.

"Five thirty?" I exclaimed. "Wow, that went by fast."

"Homework?" Mom asked as she took off her coat.

I shook my head. "Actually, I was . . . well, come see." I waited until she joined me, scooting my chair over so she could look over my shoulder. "I looked up all the therapists on that list you made," I explained, clicking from tab to tab. "And this one's a site where patients leave anonymous reviews. I've been trying to use them to narrow the choices down so we can pick a few to call, but there's just so many!"

Mom blinked several times, then turned to stare at me. "Are you okay? Did something happen?"

"What do you mean?"

"Well," Mom said slowly, "I've been asking you to do this for months, and you clearly didn't want to. Is it because you're grounded? Because, Erin, I'm happy you're open to getting back into therapy, but that's not going to make me unground—"

"No, that's not it," I interrupted. "I swear. I just . . . well, I ran into Leila's sister, Tania, today, and we talked a little and . . ." I swallowed, staring at my knees. "I think I figured out why I kept putting off finding a therapist."

Mom tilted her head. "Oh?"

"Yeah." I took a deep breath, then met her gaze. "I thought I'd outgrown panic attacks. Like they just happened because I was little and couldn't handle being stressed. But then Dad gets sent on this mission, and suddenly I'm hyperventilating in class and sleeping with Brave Bonnie Broomstick like when I was seven. So I was trying to distract myself with all this extra work because I figured that was a lot more mature. But"—I added quickly when Mom opened her mouth to protest—"Tania said getting professional help is the mature way to handle it, so." I gestured at the screen. "Therapists. Ta-da."

I slumped back in my chair with an exaggerated sigh. Mom smiled at me, her eyes suspiciously shiny. "Do *not* cry," I warned her. "I'm tired of crying. Crying is banned in this house."

Mom laughed. "Fair enough." She leaned over and planted a loud kiss on the top of my head. "I'm proud of you, sweetheart. Everything you just said? *That* was very, very mature."

I smiled. "Thanks."

"Is film club meeting tomorrow after school?"

"Yeah, definitely," I replied, ignoring a little pang of sadness. "We're into round two for the talent show, so there are a lot of videos to watch."

"If you're feeling okay," Mom began, and I held my breath. "I suppose you can go to film club. Just for an hour," she added quickly. "Then it's straight home. Okay?"

I nodded fervently. "Thank you."

"You're welcome." Mom headed into the kitchen, then turned around in the doorway. "Let me know if you need help with that, okay?" she said, pointing to the screen.

"I will." Sighing, I started scrolling through the therapist reviews again. But my mind wasn't on therapists anymore. My eyes kept straying over to my phone. No coding club group texts, which was unsurprising, given how awkward things had gotten today.

But Maya hadn't been there, I remembered suddenly, and I grabbed my phone.

> **hey!! how'd it go with hannah?**

(ER)

To my relief, Maya responded right away.

> SO FUN. i can't wait to show you these new outfits!

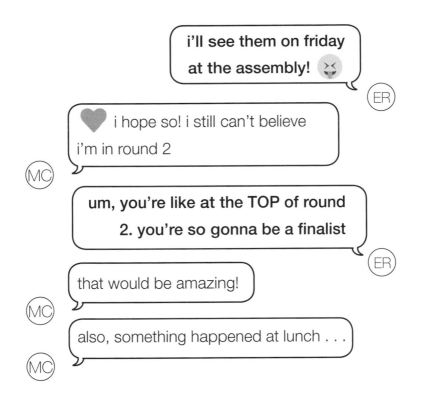

i'll see them on friday at the assembly! **ER**

i hope so! i still can't believe i'm in round 2 **MC**

um, you're like at the TOP of round 2. you're so gonna be a finalist **ER**

that would be amazing! **MC**

also, something happened at lunch . . . **MC**

My stomach twisted a little. Had one of our other friends told her about me running out of the cafeteria? The little text dots kept popping up then disappearing, and I pictured Maya typing and deleting, typing and deleting. At last, a text appeared.

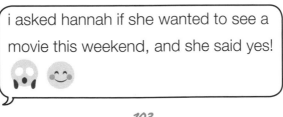

i asked hannah if she wanted to see a movie this weekend, and she said yes! **MC**

"Oh my god!"

A moment later, Mom stuck her head out of the kitchen to find me bouncing up and down in my chair, my smile ear to ear. "Everything okay?"

"Yup!" I replied, my thumbs flying over the screen.

I set my phone down, still smiling, and tried to focus on therapist reviews. But it was a lost cause. Partly because I was excited for Maya, but also because I was nervous about seeing Lucy, Sophia, and Leila tomorrow. Our group text was still unusually quiet, and things had been so tense at lunch today. Then I'd run off like a weirdo. I wanted to explain everything to them, but everyone had been so stressed out lately with robots and softball and all our different interests. Plus, at the end of this week, Mrs. Clark was leaving.

My stomach twisted as I had a terrible thought. What if this was just the beginning of the end of our coding club group?

Chapter Ten

When I got to school the next morning, it seemed like every kid I passed was staring at their phone, and the *All the Talents* web app was pulled up on every screen. Round two only had twenty contestants, and everyone was excitedly talking about their favorites. I was pleased to hear Maya's name mentioned more than once.

My excitement and anticipation seemed to double every time the bell rang. By the end of fourth period, my stomach was so full of butterflies, I didn't know if I'd even be able to eat my sandwich. I'd just stepped into the hall when I felt my phone buzz in my pocket, and I pulled it out.

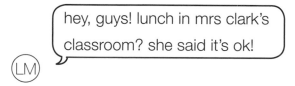

(LM)

I pressed my back against the lockers to let everyone else pass. Chewing my lip, I stared at the screen until the next text popped up.

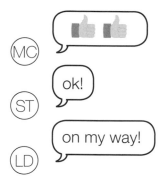

(MC)

(ST)

(LD)

I exhaled a sigh of relief and typed a reply.

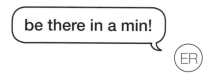

(ER)

I headed in the opposite direction of the cafeteria, the butterflies in my stomach basically swing dancing now. But I couldn't help feeling relieved, too. I had no idea why Lucy wanted us to have lunch in Mrs. Clark's room, but after what happened yesterday, I was perfectly fine with avoiding the crowded cafeteria.

Mrs. Clark was leaving just as I arrived. "Hi, Erin," she said warmly. "Just running to the cafeteria. I can't believe it's my last-ever chicken-fingers day!"

I fake gasped, placing my hand on my forehead like I was going to faint. "Wait, does TechTown not serve chicken fingers in their cafeteria? Those monsters! You should quit and stay here with us. That would teach them a lesson."

"Actually," Mrs. Clark said, raising an eyebrow. "Everyone at TechTown gets to order their lunches from their favorite restaurants. Including the Bakeshop."

My eyes widened. "So you get to eat cupcakes while you code?"

"I do," she replied, nodding seriously. "Well, as long as I keep the frosting off my keyboard."

I let out an exaggerated sigh. "Oh fine. I guess it's a pretty cool job."

Mrs. Clark winked at me. "It's pretty great. But it won't be the same, not seeing you girls every day."

"You could visit coding club sometimes," I said immediately. "And I'll bring homemade cupcakes! The Bakeshop's got nothing on my baking skills."

She laughed. "It's a deal."

I waved as she hurried down the hall, then stepped inside her room. Lucy was already there, arranging five chairs in a circle. She smiled at me, and I couldn't help thinking she looked just as nervous as I felt.

"Hi."

"Hi." I walked over, squeezing my lunch bag so hard, I crushed my chips. "So, um. What's this about?" I asked, gesturing to the chairs.

"Oh, Mrs. Clark said we can't eat near the computers."

Despite my nerves, I laughed, thinking of the cupcakes. "No, I mean why are we having lunch here instead of the cafeteria?"

"Well." Lucy shifted nervously in her seat. "I thought some privacy would be nice after, um, yesterday."

Before I could respond, Maya and Leila walked in. "Private lunch room!" Maya exclaimed, claiming a chair and stretching out her legs. "Nice."

"Yeah, we should do this every day," Leila agreed, glancing over her shoulder. "Hi, Sophia!"

"Hi." Sophia stood in the doorway, with the same nervous smile as Lucy. For some reason, realizing I wasn't the only one who was nervous made me less nervous.

Once everyone was seated, we looked at Lucy. She took a deep breath.

"Okay, so the reason I wanted us to eat in here is I thought maybe we should talk about what happened at lunch yesterday."

I swallowed hard. Then Lucy, Sophia, and I all blurted out:

"I'm sorry!"

We stared at one another, open-mouthed. After a second, Maya started chuckling. Then Leila joined in, and soon the rest of us did, too.

"Okay, hold on," Lucy said, looking at Sophia. "What are you sorry about?"

"For not helping more with everything coding club has been doing," Sophia replied. "I know you all got stuck with a lot of extra work since I've had softball tryouts, and I feel bad."

"And I've been working on my fashion show," Maya added. "I probably slacked off on coding club, too."

"I didn't do any extra work, either," Leila admitted. "I've been spending a lot of time getting ready for this robotics competition." She hesitated, giving me an uncertain look. "And Erin got stuck testing the site all by herself. Tania said you were really stressed out, Erin. I'm so sorry."

Now everyone was looking at me.

"It's okay," I said. "I volunteered for all that. Work zombie, remember." I looked down at my hands. "But that plan kind of backfired on me. I was trying to distract myself from something."

I paused, glancing at Maya, and she smiled encouragingly. Then I told my friends all about my dad's missions and my panic attacks.

"I had one on Saturday when Maya came over to help me with my video," I finished. "That's the real reason I dropped out of the talent show."

Exhaling loudly, I leaned back in my chair. No tightness in my chest, no super-fast pulse, no sweaty hands. The only thing I felt was relieved.

Lucy spoke first. "Erin, I'm *so* sorry," she said, her eyes wide and round. "I had no idea. And I kept asking you for help with the teacher app, too!"

Leila reached over and patted my arm. "Is there anything *we* can do to distract you?"

"Yeah!" Sophia said eagerly. "Want us to come over after school? We could watch a movie or something!"

"We could bake cookies!" Lucy added.

Maya sat up straight. "Two words: dance party."

"*Three* words," Leila chimed in. "Robot dance party."

Warmth radiated in my chest as my friends

continued suggesting increasingly goofy ways to distract me. I couldn't believe that I'd ever been worried about our friendship falling apart without coding club.

"Okay, it's settled," I announced. "Friday after school, you're all coming over for the movie-cookie-robot-dance-party-athon of the century!"

"Perfect!" Leila said. "And we can celebrate Maya winning the talent show, because we all know she's going to."

Maya fiddled with the silver star charm on her necklace. "Ha, we'll see. But I'd love to come over!"

Sophia nodded. "Me too!"

I turned to Lucy and was surprised to see she looked a little teary. "What's wrong?" I asked, alarmed.

She smiled and blinked a ton, staring up at the ceiling. "Nothing! It's just ... well, I know this is going to sound silly, but ever since Mrs. Clark told us she's leaving, I've been worried that ..."

I stared at her, realization dawning. "That we'd all stop being friends?"

Lucy shrugged. "Yeah, kind of. Everyone was suddenly so busy with other stuff . . . it felt like everything was changing. I think that's why I've been so obsessed with the teacher app. I guess I thought if I found the perfect replacement for Mrs. Clark, you wouldn't quit the club."

"Quit?!" Maya placed her hand over her heart dramatically. "Never!"

"No way!" Sophia agreed. "And, Lucy, even if there was no coding club, you know we'd all still be friends."

Lucy looked at all of us, teary-eyed. "I know. It was silly of me."

"No, it wasn't," I told her. "I was worried about the same thing!"

"Really?"

"Yeah, I was totally afraid we were drifting apart or something." I paused. "I think that's part of why I've been so anxious. My old therapist did say clubs were helpful, but I don't think it's because they distract you from what's making you anxious. It's because they help you make friends who can help you when you need it."

"Like when you have a ton of chores to do if you want to make it to the hackathon on time," Sophia said. We all laughed at the memory, but I knew Sophia was right. We were more than teammates. We were friends, and friends are there to help when you need it the most.

Lucy looked at me curiously. "So do you have a therapist now? It sounds like your old one was pretty cool."

"She was," I said with a loud sigh. "I've been looking for a new one, but it's so . . . ughhhhhhh." I slumped over in my chair, letting my arms dangle, and my friends giggled.

"Why is it *ughh*?" Maya asked.

"There are just so many to choose from, and all these reviews, and every time I try to go through them all, it's really overwhelming."

I opened my lunch bag, then realized Lucy was still staring at me. But now she had a familiar glint in her eyes.

"Can you send me a link to those reviews?" she asked. "I think I have an idea . . ."

Chapter Eleven

The instant my alarm went off Friday morning, I stumbled out of bed and hurried to my computer. Out of habit, I glanced at Dad's dot—gray, of course—then pulled up *All the Talents*. The twenty finalists' videos were on the front page, and after I logged in, the voting options appeared below each one.

Squinting, I found Maya's video and clicked the thumbs-up on the criteria below it. Then I started voting on the other videos. Since film club had gone through all twenty already, I didn't need to watch them again. I had five to go when Mom poked her head in the door.

"I don't think I've ever witnessed this before," she mused, cradling a mug of coffee in her hands. "My daughter, Erin Roberts, actually getting up when her alarm goes off, instead of hitting snooze a dozen times."

"Ha ha," I said dryly, clicking on one of my favorite videos—Sarah Rodriguez's Claymation film. "Voting on the next round started this morning, and I want to make sure our site is working okay."

"When are the top three announced?" Mom asked.

"Voting closes at noon," I replied. "Then the site should send everyone an e-mail with the results."

"Very cool!" Mom sipped some of her coffee. "I wonder if any other school talent show has ever had so much talent behind the scenes."

I grinned. "Probably not." I had to admit, she was right. I was still sad that I'd missed out on actually entering the talent show, but putting it together had been a fun new experience for me. I was always so focused on being onstage, I'd never actually realized what exactly went on offstage.

After I finished voting, I got dressed and ate breakfast in record time. When I got to school, I saw Hannah standing outside the entrance.

"Oh hey, Erin!" She waved her phone excitedly. "Did you vote already?"

"Of course!" I exclaimed. "I hope you're ready to

walk the runway this afternoon."

Hannah gave me a conspiratorial grin. "Oh, I am. Actually . . ." She glanced around, then leaned closer. "Don't tell Maya, but Ms. Davies let me store all the outfits Maya made for the talent show in the theater club room."

"All of them?" I repeated. "But you're her only model!"

"Not anymore." Hannah was so excited, she was almost hopping in place. "I've been asking all of Maya's coding club friends to model. Lucy and Leila already said yes, and I called Sophia last night—she's bringing that amazing dress Maya made her for the dance last semester. So . . . are you in?"

"Oh wow, of course! So the plan is to surprise her?"

"Yes, exactly!"

"Cool." I mimed zipping my lips and throwing the key down the hallway. "I won't say a word."

Hannah beamed at me. "Thanks, Erin!"

We walked through the double doors, then waved and headed in opposite directions. I felt a surge of pride every time I passed another student with *All the Talents* pulled up on their phone.

Even my teachers kept getting distracted by the

talent show during class. Mr. Hupton, my history teacher, spent almost fifteen minutes speculating with us over who would be in the top three. By the time the bell rang for lunch a few minutes before noon, the atmosphere throughout the whole school felt like it was crackling with anticipation.

I walked to the cafeteria with my eyes glued to my phone, refreshing my e-mail inbox over and over. Then, just as I reached the cafeteria, an e-mail titled *All the Talents: FINALISTS!* popped up, and I almost walked into the wall. I opened it quickly, my stomach doing cartwheels.

Congratulations again to everyone who made it into round two of *All the Talents*! The votes are in, and your top three finalists, in no particular order, are:

Sarah Rodriguez

Kyle Ward

Maya Chung

The finalists will perform at this afternoon's assembly. Immediately afterward, log in to *All the Talents* to vote for your favorite contestant!

I did a little happy dance right there in the hall, then hurried into the cafeteria. Maya wasn't there yet, but Lucy, Leila, and Sophia were already at our table. They beamed at me as I sat down and raised my arms in a V for victory.

"You ladies ready to be models?" I said.

"*Yes!*" Lucy squirmed in her seat, still tapping her phone screen. "I'm so psyched for Maya!"

"I can't wait to see what we're actually modeling!" Leila exclaimed. "Hannah said they were working on something really cool."

"I can't imagine anything cooler than the dress she made for me," Sophia said, her eyes shining.

"Hey, Erin." Lucy swiped her screen again, then turned to me. "Ta-da!" She held her phone out, and I saw what looked like the teacher app she'd been working on.

"Oh, you finished it!" I said. "So who's the ideal teacher?"

Lucy shook her head. "No idea. This is something different."

Confused, I took her phone and started scrolling down the page. The names weren't any that I recognized as teachers. But they were familiar. After a few seconds, I realized why.

"These are the therapists from my mom's list!"

"Exactly!" Lucy beamed. "When you said all the reviews were overwhelming, I got this idea. These reviews are just data, right? People saying what they liked or didn't like about the therapist . . . exactly like what I was going to do with the teacher app. So I just changed the criteria to stuff relevant to therapists, had the app analyze the data, and voilà!"

I blinked in amazement as I continued to scroll. Beneath every therapist was a list of qualities like timeliness, kindness, and listening skills. And next to each was a rating between one and five, averaged from their patients' reviews.

"Lucy," I said slowly. "This is . . . wow." Setting her phone down, I leaned over and hugged her. "Thank you *so* much."

"So you think it'll make it easier for you to pick one?" she asked eagerly, and I nodded.

"Absolutely."

"*Eek*, there's Maya!" Sophia said, pointing. Then she lowered her voice to a whisper. "Omigod. It's going to be so hard to keep this fashion show thing a secret for the rest of the day! What if Maya notices we're acting weird?"

"Don't worry," I replied, glancing at Hannah as she hurried across the cafeteria and threw her arms around a blushing Maya. "I think she already has plenty of distractions today."

Near the end of fifth period, all talent show contestants were called to the auditorium. I sprinted to the theater club's dressing room, nearly colliding with Leila and Lucy when I rounded the last corner.

"Is she here yet?" I gasped, clutching my sides.

"Not yet!" Lucy held the door open, and we hurried inside. Hannah was already there, fussing over a rack with five outfits.

"Quick!" she said, waving us over. "Everyone pick an outfit before Maya gets here."

"She's supposed to check in with the teachers in the auditorium first," I said, grabbing an outfit off the rack. "That should give us a few minutes!"

Sophia slipped into the room, clutching a garment bag. "I saw Maya and had to hide," she huffed, and we laughed. Lucy, Leila, and Hannah chose their outfits, and soon we were all oohing and ahhing over our Maya Chung originals.

"This fabric is so pretty," Lucy said. Her romper was

covered in a print of bright yellow butterflies.

"I know," I agreed, holding my hanger out at arm's length. I'd picked palazzo pants and a matching scoop-neck top in a galaxy print, black with clusters of white, pink, and purple stars. Leila had chosen a chocolate-brown jumpsuit with a swirly pattern in almost the exact same shade of turquoise as her head scarf. And Hannah's ankle-length, full-skirted dress looked like flames—dark red at the bottom that faded into orange in the middle and yellow at her shoulders. She was already wearing a light yellow headband that matched the dress perfectly.

"You'll look like a walking flame emoji," I told her. "And I mean that in the best possible way."

Hannah laughed. "Thanks!" she said, just as the door opened and Maya walked in.

"Oh!" Her eyes widened in surprise, and she clapped her hands over her mouth. "What are you all doing here?"

"I asked them to model!" Hannah told her, beaming. "It'd be a total tragedy if the whole school didn't get to see *all* the new outfits you've been working on."

"Wow." Maya looked at each of us in turn, her eyes shiny. "That's . . . you're the best."

"Can we put these on already?" Leila said, shaking her jumpsuit excitedly.

"Yes! Go!"

We cheered, and everyone quickly started to dress. Leila finished first, then helped Sophia adjust the battery pack on her shoulder.

"Hey, Maya," Sophia called. "Do you want me to turn on the lights in my dress? I don't know if anyone will be able to see them under the stage lights."

Maya and Hannah shared a look. "Actually," Maya said slowly. "I guess I should warn you all about that."

"I've already talked to the theater-club girl running the lights," Hannah explained. "After we each walk down the runway, we'll line up at the edge of the stage. Then she's going to turn off all the lights."

"Why? Does Hannah's dress light up, too?" I squinted at Hannah, as if her dress was embedded with invisible LED lights.

"Not exactly. But . . ." Maya pressed her lips together. "Well, we had some fun picking out the fabric. You'll see."

Lucy and I gave each other puzzled looks, and Leila peered curiously at Hannah's dress. The door opened again, and Ms. Davies stuck in her head. "Girls? Are you ready?"

"Let's do this!" I cheered, and we followed Ms. Davies backstage. We lined up on the left side of the stage, Hannah in the lead, and watched as Ms. Davies and Maya slipped through the curtains. A moment later, the chatter in the auditorium turned to applause, and my stomach fluttered with nerves—the good kind. The performing kind.

Ms. Davies's voice rang through the speakers as she introduced Maya and explained that she had designed and sewn every outfit the audience was about to see. A moment later, a loud pop song started to play, the thumping of the bass matching the thumping in my chest.

"Here we go!" Hannah called, standing up tall and smiling widely. She stepped through the curtains, and the cheers doubled in volume.

Lucy followed after a few seconds, then Sophia, then Leila. Taking a deep breath, I swaggered onto the stage after her.

I could barely see the kids in the auditorium, but I could definitely hear them. Overhead, lights in at least a dozen different colors were flashing. So were the lights sewn into Sophia's dress, although she was right—they were barely visible. Once we each had strutted down the runway, we lined up at the edge of the stage. The beat stopped, and the song turned to a long, dramatic drone. Then the lights turned off, and the whole auditorium was black.

"Whoa!" I cried, staring down at my outfit. The white, pink, and purple galaxies were glowing in the dark, sparkling like real stars. I turned to look at Lucy and Leila—their patterns were glow-in-the-dark, too, and Sophia's flashing LED lights were now impossible to miss. And at the other end of the line, Hannah's entire dress glowed, including her headband. She really did look like a walking flame emoji!

Laughing, we all struck poses while the crowd cheered and whistled. Then the stage lights came back on, the beat kicked in again, and we danced offstage to the right. The second Maya joined us, we tackled her in a group hug.

"That was amazing!" I yelled, grabbing Maya's arm and lifting it triumphantly in the air. "Ladies and gentlemen, may I present the winner of *All the Talents*!"

Maya ducked her head, giggling. Her face was flushed, her eyes all shiny again. "Thank you all *so* much," she said. "I honestly don't care what place I get.

It was so amazing to see you modeling my outfits!"

Ms. Davies's voice sounded through the speakers again, and we all fell silent as she introduced Sarah Rodriguez. A few seconds later, Sarah's Claymation film started. I'd watched it at least a dozen times—it was a cool, slightly creepy story about a puppet coming to life—and I could hear the crowd oohing and aahing when it appeared on the giant projector screen over the stage. I high-fived Sarah when she joined the rest of us, and Ms. Davies brought out Kyle Ward, who put on what I had to admit was a really impressive dancing magic act. Then Kyle huddled backstage with us, and the whole auditorium fell silent.

"You've seen the finalists," Ms. Davies said. "Now it's time to vote! You can use your phone if you have one, or use one of the tablets set up in the aisles or the back of the auditorium. Go to the *All the Talents* web app, log in with your student ID, and you'll see the names of these three finalists on the home page. Just tap on your favorite, and you're done!"

I stuck my head through the curtain. All over the auditorium, students' faces glowed under the lights of phones and tablets. A second later, Lucy poked my arm.

"We need to vote, too!"

"Oh yeah!"

The six of us raced across the hall to the theater-club dressing room to grab our phones. There were a few seconds of silence as we all pulled up the site and voted—using the feature we had designed!

"You'd all better be voting for Maya," Hannah said sternly, and everyone laughed. Once we were finished, we headed back to the auditorium to wait for the results to be announced. While my friends chatted away, I kept sticking my head through the curtains to see if everyone was done voting. Finally, I saw Ms. Davies step behind the microphone holding a tablet, and I waved frantically at the others.

"Here we go!" I hissed, and Maya scrunched up her face like she was holding her breath.

"Once again, thanks to everyone who entered *All the Talents* this year!" Ms. Davies said. "I think we can all agree, this was one of the most impressive talent shows we've ever had. And now, if the finalists will join me onstage?"

Maya walked out onstage with Kyle and Sarah, and I screamed my head off along with everyone else. Hannah stuck her fingers between her lips and let out a piercing whistle that caused Lucy to shriek and the rest of us to burst out laughing.

The cheers died down as Ms. Davies made a show of swiping her tablet.

"In second place," she said. "Maya Chung!"

Beaming, Maya stepped forward to accept her ribbon from Ms. Davies. My friends and I cheered at the top of our lungs until Maya joined us backstage, and Hannah gave her a huge hug.

"And the winner of this year's *All the Talents* . . ." Ms. Davies paused for dramatic effect, and a nervous gasp escaped my throat. "Sarah Rodriguez!"

The cheers were deafening as Sarah stepped forward with a huge grin to accept her trophy. Even though I'd wanted Maya to win, I was thrilled for Sarah, too.

"Last year's talent show didn't have any fashion shows or films," I told Lucy over the applause. "I hope we do this format next year, too."

Lucy gave me a slightly shifty smile. "I may have already started a list of ideas for improving the app," she admitted.

I gasped. "Oh my god. Are you okay? Do you need a doctor?"

"What? Why?" Lucy asked, her eyes wide.

"Because I think you've been bitten by . . ." I stuck my arms out straight and groaned. *"Woooork zombiiieee . . ."*

Lucy shrieked and ran off, and the others cracked up as I lumbered after her.

Chapter Twelve

"*Nom.*" Sophia grabbed a double-chocolate-chip cookie right off the rack and crammed it into her mouth.

"They haven't cooled off yet," I warned, then chortled when her eyes bugged out. Lucy handed her a glass of milk, and Sophia chugged it, crumbs falling from her mouth as she did.

Over at the kitchen table, Maya was laying out rolls of the glow-in-the-dark fabric she'd used to make our dresses. Leila sat next to her, reading something on her phone. Just as the timer went off for my second batch of cookies, Leila said, "Aha!" and held out her phone for Maya to read.

"Oh, that looks pretty easy!" Maya said eagerly. "Hey, Erin, can I borrow some scissors?"

"Sure!" I pulled them out of the drawer and handed them to her. "What are you making?"

Leila pointed to the star-covered fabric Maya had used for my dress. "A galaxy head scarf for me! And one for Tania, although I'm not sure which pattern she'd like best."

I set the sheet of piping hot cookies on the counter, then turned to look at the fabrics. "The fire one from Hannah's dress," I said decisively, and Leila nodded.

"Yeah, you're right. She'll love it."

Ping! Ping! Ping! Ping! Ping!

We all fell silent, staring at one another. "Did we *all* just get a text at the same time?" Lucy wondered, pulling her phone out of her pocket.

"Maybe someone hacked into our group text," I joked, taking out my phone. Then I blinked in surprise. "Oh wow—it's from Mrs. Clark!"

Hi, girls! Just wanted to say congratulations—not just to Maya, but to you all.

The talent show wouldn't have been such a success without the super-talented coding club!

"Aw, I'm going to miss her so much," Lucy said. Then she squinted at her screen. "Oh wait . . . she's typing another message."

 Also, TechTown has a few fun apps in the works, and they're looking for teens and tweens to act as beta testers. I told them I just might know a few. 😉 I'll be in touch!

 ps Erin, don't forget your promise 🧁🧁🧁🧁🧁🧁

"Whoa!" I cried, and the others looked just as excited. "That is so cool!"

We all spent the next few minutes bombarding

Mrs. Clark with texts and talking about how amazing it would be to beta test a brand-new app.

"I wonder what kind of apps they are," Leila said. "Maybe Tania can tell us more about them."

"I hope one is a karaoke app," I said. "Or some sort of voice-effect app. Ooh, I would have *so* much fun with that . . ."

Sophia helped herself to another cookie. "You know, Erin," she said around a mouthful. "I'm still pretty bummed we never got to see you perform that song. Maya said you even had a stuffed monkey."

"It's true," I said. "Actually, I think it's still in my room."

Lucy gasped. "Omigod, Erin. Can you *please* put on that performance for us?"

"Yes!" Sophia cried, and Leila nodded fervently. I noticed Maya giving me a worried glance before she cleared her throat.

"Guys, maybe that's not such a good idea . . ."

"No, it's fine!" I said, and she looked at me uncertainly. "Seriously."

"Oh wait." Lucy slapped her forehead. "I'm sorry—I totally forgot it gave you a panic attack last time."

"It's fine!" I said again, and I meant it. Just talking to

my friends about my dad was already helping me feel less anxious. Plus, after that assembly this afternoon, I was craving another performance.

We piled all the cookies onto a few plates, grabbed our glasses of milk, and headed for my room. "Are you ladies still my backup crew?" I asked as I flipped on my keyboard.

"*Yes,*" Maya said, grabbing the stuffed monkey. "But don't be mad when I end up laughing too hard to sing or dance."

She threw me the monkey, and I found the accompaniment on the keyboard. Just as I was about to hit play, there was a knock at my door.

"Come in!" I called. Mom opened the door, her eyebrows quirking up at the sight of my friends in a straight line in front of my bed, mouths smudged with cookie crumbs. "You're just in time," I said grandly, waving the stuffed monkey. "I'm about to put on the performance of the century."

Mom's eyes twinkled. "This *is* perfect timing. I happen to have someone here who would love to watch."

She stepped all the way into my room, and I realized she was holding her laptop. And on the screen was a familiar, if slightly sunburned, face smiling at me from under an army cap. For a moment, I froze, so surprised I couldn't even react. Then my dad's voice came through the tiny laptop speakers.

"Hi, sweetie!"

"Dad!" I cried, my eyes instantly welling up with happy tears. I flew across the room and hugged the laptop, and Mom and Dad both laughed. Stepping back, I wiped my cheeks and beamed at him. "You're okay? The mission's over?"

"Yes and yes," he said, then tilted his head. "But we can talk about that later. I believe I was about to see the performance of the century?"

Behind me, my friends giggled. I held up the stuffed monkey, and waited until Dad's eyes lit up with recognition.

"I really *did* call at the perfect time!" He struck a robot-like dance pose. "Hope you girls don't mind if I join the dance party."

"You'd better," I said as my friends chuckled again. Hurrying back over to the keyboard, I looked around at them eagerly.

"Ready?"

"Yes!" Sophia exclaimed just as Maya said, "Noooo,"

and Lucy and Leila covered their mouths with their hands to stifle their laughter.

I lifted my chin and adopted an imperious expression, clapping my hands briskly. "Places, girls!"

They hurried to stand in a straight line. Sophia grabbed the last bit of cookie from Lucy's hand, and Lucy gasped in pretend outrage. But Leila stole it from Sophia and gave her a mock-stern look before handing the cookie to Maya, who shrugged and popped it into her mouth. As they acted silly and poked one another, I felt as light as a helium balloon, ready to float to the ceiling. Lucy, Sophia, Maya, and Leila might have started out as my coding club friends, but they were my best friends now, and I knew nothing would change that.

I hit play on the keyboard. Mom leaned against my bedroom door, holding the laptop for Dad to see as I took my place in the middle of my room. The opening chords sounded, and I stared deeply into the stuffed monkey's eyes.

"I know you don't think so, but it's tru-u-ue . . ."

Behind me, Sophia and Leila sang along loudly, but Maya and Lucy were already cracking up. I dipped the monkey like we were ballroom dancing.

"I can move, I can dance, better than you-u-u..."

Mom and Dad were starting to laugh, too, but I was in total performance mode now. The synthesized drumbeat I'd programmed kicked in, and I danced like a short-circuiting robot, flailing and twitching and spinning while Mom, Dad, and my best friends cheered me on.

Don't miss these other Girls Who Code books!